Serpents of Sky

Nine stories of dragons

by Heidi C. Vlach

May you always have wings to fly on.

HCVlach

Copyright 2014 Heidi C. Vlach

Published by Heidi C. Vlach. All rights reserved.

All characters appearing in this work are fictitious. Any resemblance to real persons, living or dead, is purely coincidental.

ISBN 978-0-9869390-6-8

www.heidicvlach.com

Table of Contents

With Less Lament	1
Mistaken	13
Cardiology	17
Clearsight	33
Iron Workings	47
Another Odyssey	59
In Lifetimes Spared	65
An introduction to the Stories of Aligare	81
The Korvi's Limbs	83
Raise (A story of Aligare)	89

Foreword

I've always found dragons fascinating — and I'm not alone. Since before recorded history, worldwide cultures have been imagining up monsters, guardians and deities that can all be named "dragon". It seems like the concept strikes some particularly meaningful note in the human mind.

This collection of short stories is my way of mounting an expedition. I'm exploring the concept of dragons. Exploring them as gods, as beasts, and as relatable loved ones. I hope you'll enjoy the sights along the way.

HCVlach

The earth is a tangle of dragons.

— Genevieve Valentine

With Less Lament

In any time of fright, Eloise found it comforting to get her hands into the soil. Turning in a bit of fertilizer helped her rose bushes. Touching the earth kept her mind off the sky.

She looked to the sky anyway; the dragon advisory on the morning radio broadcast seemed louder each time she thought of it.

Citizens are advised to keep calm and practice positive thinking. Avoid discussion of political events, religion and other divisive topics unless vitally necessary. In case of dragon sighting, seek shelter immediately.

She sighted only blue sky and clouds overhead. And she didn't talk about news stories or church, anyway. Eloise brushed her arthritis-bent fingers clean on her apron and stayed sitting in her garden. Coral-pink roses wagged, with bees humming between them. The breeze wafted by, warm as a full teacup but still a relief from summer's heat. It had been a lovely day so far today — now, if only everyone could enjoy the outdoors and stop feeding the sky devil.

No use thinking of that. The dragon was as inevitable as rain, or taxes. Eloise began to hum, aimlessly at first but then catching hold of a lively little swing tune. Her own voice filled her ears and the garden was alive around her. More bees hovered drunk between the flowers; that bold, red-throated hummingbird arrived, zipping over to a morning glory blossom hanging from the lattice. Digging more carefully — like she

2

might bother the little darling with any human movement — Eloise kept up the tune. She had never heard of hummingbirds being especially friendly but this one was. He came closer sometimes, to buzz in the air and stare at her before darting away. It was nice to think that he liked a bit of music, too.

The hummingbird paused in front of her today. Not to stare at Eloise, though. More like he was listening for something. She hummed the chorus twice before she noticed: some omen hung in the air, a change in the weight of the day. She pushed off the warm grass, her joints all scolding together. Maybe she should check the radio, she thought, in case there was a new bulletin.

Then the wind turned. It reeked of oily smoke.

Too late for a bulletin. Eloise had to get somewhere safe. Had to get to the dragon shelter in the basement — those cinder block walls that Herbert laid, God rest his soul. Eloise couldn't run these days: she could only hurry her shuffling walk toward the porch steps that looked a mile away. The sky devil roared overhead, tearing the air like a thunderstorm.

She reached the porch door, the latch giving under her clumsy hands. Yes, be grateful for that, Eloise knew. Think kind thoughts and graceful emotions. Bad feelings fed the terror beast — but no one ever said good feelings couldn't drive it away, so God willing, maybe it was true.

She was at the basement stairs when the dragon struck, a screaming of wood and plaster. The house shook. Eloise was falling, grabbing for the door frame. The world came down.

She woke to darkness and hot-glowing pain. The dragon had finally come for her. Maybe she was in the next life, Eloise thought. She stayed unmoving, breathing in the taste of dust and wood and acrid ruin.

Something crackled at the far edge of her awareness. Eloise held her breath and welled up with terror, and felt bathwater tears on her face, and listened. More crackling sounds, like the house's shambles being dragged aside. It didn't sound like the dragon: whatever made the noise was plainly too small for that. Maybe someone come to rescue her, then.

"Help," Eloise croaked, small under everything. "Please. I'm here!" Crackling, crackling. It didn't sound like a fireman's axe or a jaws-of-life machine. More like someone powerful was bending the entire house with mighty hands.

Against her howling headache, Eloise turned her head. Light poured in wider with each crackle, with each shifting of debris that used to be her house. There weren't any people coming for her — just a tiny dark spot in flight. A hummingbird. A tiny hummingbird in midair, thrumming closer.

"How did you," Eloise breathed.

It tipped its head; light caught on feathers so fine they looked like fish scales. This was her red-throated friend.

More rubble crackled, this time above and around Eloise. Weight lifted off her and pain surged into her legs. She needed to get out, said a thought like a blunt nudge. Find shelter, safety.

She certainly didn't want to die here, she knew as she crawled toward white light. She didn't want to die at all. The hummingbird zipped away and hung in the dust-glittering air, waiting, watching her. Eloise lost sight of it as she coughed, as she dragged forward inches at a time.

Soon, the dirt and shambles were gone and Eloise reached dust-covered grass. She kept going, gasping in the daylight. She stopped when the deep breathing started to pinch inside her. Her friend still hung in the air on blurring wings, watching her. Eloise looked up at the whirring sound and maybe it was a trick of the light, but he had a presence in his eyes, a gleam nearly like intelligence.

You-well-are?

4

A voice — but Eloise couldn't tell where it had come from. She only knew that she heard it, clear as a glass bell. She turned on sore bones and couldn't see anyone, no rescuers — only rubble and shattered lattice and a gouge in the driveway. Her eyes caught on that: a cut through the asphalt, a good five feet down into the earth. That must have been from the dragon's claws. It had claws like big hooks, people said. The devil was built to kill.

A sudden sense of frustration, like a glimpse of someone else's heart. Then Eloise heard the voice again, saying *are you alright?*

"I-I'm—" She looked back to the hummingbird, the glittering jewel fixed in the air.

Yes. You see correctly.

"I-I—" She gulped down a sound she might have made. "My head hurts. And my legs, too. Am I dead?"

He tilted his head. *No. I hope you won't soon be dead. You need to come with me. This way.*

The hummingbird zipped ten feet away and kept staring at her. Ten feet that would be too far to walk on a bad arthritis day, never mind now. Eloise put a hand to her face, found it still wet and rubbed at it. "I-I don't think I can ..."

You can. You must live. Please, hurry — before the beast returns.

He hovered over the plainest corner of the backyard, some simple crabgrass and azalea branches. There was no safety there. Yet the voice in Eloise's head seemed so sure. She gathered her fistful of strength and she pulled herself further inches.

Long minutes passed, making small bites of progress between the shrieking of her body. Eloise gripped at the grass now, soothing even though her palms were filmed with dust.

This might be close enough, the hummingbird said. He flitted away, closer to the azalea bushes.

Eloise only closed her eyes for a moment, long enough to smear her tears away with the wrinkled back of her hand. But in that moment, something passed over her, warm as daylight. She was suddenly facing more hummingbirds, dozens of rainbow-feathered little creatures sitting on the grass and buzzing in the air. Most of them stared at her with the very same understanding eyes.

You are shielded, her red-throated friend said, plain and proud. He flitted upward — and there was no sky overhead now, just a shimmering dome that swirled with gold hues when he tapped it with his beak. *None will find us here!*

An unseeable place: that thought sat leaden in Eloise's gut and she was too confused to say why. "I'm ... Are you an angel?"

He tilted his head again, and a realization splashed against Eloise's thoughts. *Oh, I still resemble a flitter-bird! Kyeh!*

Eloise was falling — a downward jolt of her senses. Like nearly falling asleep and catching her head mid-bob. When she blinked it away, her headache burned hotter but something different now hovered before her. A creature with slower-beating wings than a hummingbird, wings more like a bat's. He was sleek-shaped like a salamander, with spines on its head and feathers for clothes. He looked like a pretty Christmas ornament come to life and he still stared at her with dark, thinking eyes.

It is necessary to use a glamour on ourselves, so we can hide. You saw-knew me as a flitter-bird. You like those birds, yes?

"They're beautiful," Eloise agreed. "You ... you must be an angel."

The strange sensation fluttered in her again — confusion as mild as milk.

6

Kree, it doesn't matter. You are hurt. His voice shifted into a hum Eloise could barely understand, distant like someone speaking on the telephone in the other room.

One creature — who hovered nearer than the others already — buzzed toward her and landed on her shoulder. Such a slight weight that she could barely feel it through her blouse. Then the headache began to drain, and her pain eased away into blue nothingness.

We can fix your body, her friend said. *Flesh, wood, metal: they are almost the same. But we cannot fix your crying ...*

Eloise gulped and found some composure. "You're very kind," she said. "I just ... I don't understand."

The creatures looked to one another; foreign thoughts and feelings flashed past in droves. Some of the little creatures turned away, busying themselves with glittering objects in their delicate foot-hands. Some kept watching Eloise, with considering looks cast at her hovering friend.

You are not dead, he said. *And you are not seeing untruths. We live beside humans and cultivate the things you cannot understand. We are the—*

The word he used glanced off Eloise's mind, three syllables that just wouldn't fit. She was thinking suddenly of the stale smell of library books. The heraldry book she read once, full of thickly inked symbols from Eloise's own European ancestry. One shape stood clear in her mind: a proudly snarling dragon creature that pulled toward the word escaping from her now.

"Wh ... Wyvern?" she murmured.

A crinkling of emotions, like her friend was frowning and smiling together. He said it again.

"Vyverna ...?"

Near enough, he grumbled.

Another voice nudged in, weary but pleased. *Finished-I-am. Hurt-banished-is.* The scant weight on Eloise's back fluttered and was gone.

That vyverna really had banished the pain: she felt worlds better. Lighter, cleaner. Like she had slept the restoring sleep of a young woman. Eloise shifted her legs and watched them move, veined and spotted under tattered pantyhose but still legs she was grateful to have.

"Thank you," she said. "But ... why?"

Her friend drifted lower, and landed on his little foot-hands in the dust-topped grass. Craning his sleek body, he looked up at Eloise — and into her, and through her. *You won't have to cry anymore.*

They weren't people, not in the usual way. They had feelings somewhere in them but did they even know what crying was?

Yes, they did, Eloise recalled. She had sat in her garden with spade and fertilizer and she had showed them what crying was, those first weeks after she lost Herbert.

Truth, her friend agreed. His gaze was steady.

"That's why the hummingbirds liked my roses and morning glories so much ..."

Not your flower-plants. Your singing. His presence squirmed against Eloise's mind, like searching for words they shared. *This shield protecting us, and the healing in your bones ... We are stronger when song is in the air. You feed us in your garden-place. We can use that pureness of soul-feeling to strike at our dragon.*

"What?" Eloise blurted. "You have a dragon, too?"

8

He made a sound through his mouth — a trill that made the others turn toward him in rippling surprise.

The dragon, the one that almost crush-killed you. Humans think the dragon is human-made! His speech faded briefly beyond words, a frustrated buzzing. *Blind-eyed fools. How can the dragon be human-made? You have put eyesight on the dragon, have you not? Or on your photopictures of the dragon?*

She had. Eloise knew of blurry newsreels and photographs, soaked into her mind even blurrier but still distinct enough to scare her. And then last month, the six o'clock news showed a computer-generated picture of the dragon, crisp-looking, ugly as all sin. It looked like a huge, clawed salamander with horns on its head, and webbed wings, and black pits for eyes. Like a devil-wrought form of this little friend sitting in front of Eloise now.

"No," she breathed.

The dragon is vyverna-made, the rolled-together monster of all our fears and fights. The dragon shows that truth in its body-shape. All this destruction, the loss of your home and the risk to your body-life: these are troubles you can credit to the vyverna.

That couldn't be. Dragons were the oldest fairy tale creatures around, the most fearful enemies of human heroes — and fairy tales had truth in them, didn't they? People wouldn't tell their children about Saint George and the dragon if it was someone else's monster to slay. And besides, these kind little creatures weren't anything like the sky devil. Eloise tried not to frown at her friend — but he couldn't be right.

"I'm not sure about that," she said.

Frah. It does not change our seeking-initiative, the fact of where the dragon came from. Eh-lo-ise. He thought her name like pressing keys on an instrument he didn't know how to play. *We vyverna have helped you. We ask for your help given back.*

"I— Yes. Of course." She was laden with guilt, suddenly, for arguing over nothing.

We will protect you from more sky-harm, and we can repel the dragon this day. But we are few. We need fuel. Please sing for us.

What an odd time to want a song — in the middle of smoke and ruins, while the devil could still come back. But Eloise smoothed her dirt-smeared skirt and she sat there in the safe quiet, the fire truck sirens a muffled beat beyond the shining dome. She sat on grass and earth, the only real constants in her life; she was just one old woman with some tunes and tomes inside her.

She sang, quavering and small. Sang her favourite swing tune from when she was sixteen years old. Her small friend's relief came, a feeling wrapping her up like a downy coat.

It grew easier as she fell into the music. Lively songs carried themselves. The slower love songs made her think of Herbert, and those ones didn't need to be carried at all. The gathered vyverna watched her with wise beads of eyes, arriving and leaving and bustling. Their conversations were a burbling beyond Eloise's understanding but she hardly noticed beyond her songs' lyrics.

When her voice began to rasp, she hummed instead. The vyverna bustled quicker yet calmer. They connected with Eloise's friend one by one, the many threads of a nearly-real web.

10

Human voices penetrated the dome now — the shouting voices of stout men searching the rubble of Eloise's home.

She stopped, and bowed her head. "I'm sorry. They're looking for me, my family must be worried ..."

We are stronger now, her little friend said. His salamander face was smooth and unchanging but Eloise thought she saw emotion in it, a happier angle to his eyes. *We will face our enemy this day.*

Eloise flinched; a work boot fell beside her hand, distant through the dome but still only inches away. She curled that hand to her chest and found that she was tired and hungry, and so very present inside her trembling self. "Be careful," she told them. "The dragon is dangerous, wherever it came from."

We will adventure-fly with great care. Thank you, Eh-lo-ise. Be well.

She rose uneasily, and the dome allowed her through. Standing on her own slushy legs, Eloise caught her head from bobbing — and then she was standing alone in tattered clothes, looking at the collapsed husk that used to be her house. Workers and firemen and neighbours swarmed around it like ants.

One of them shouted. Faces turned all toward her.

She pushed her legs forward and found them beginning to ache again.

She listened to radio news reports, that night she spent in the emergency shelter, wrapped in a thin but well-meant blanket. One soothing-voiced anchorman said that the dragon had ravaged the entire tri-state area today, in the worst attack in decades. Hundreds dead. Billions of dollars in damages. But suddenly, it had begun acting strangely; it had thrashed far above the city like it felt a sword in its flesh; it roared and clawed at the air. Then it vanished. Returned to wherever it stayed when it wasn't menacing humanity.

Returned to Hell, Eloise thought. But she was less sure of that than she had been yesterday.

She asked one of the nice young volunteers for a cup of tea. Eloise missed her garden already; she wondered when she could get back to it and see if her rose bushes were alright, if any coral-pink blossoms were left in the ruins.

She pulled the blanket tight around her. Just in case anyone was listening, she hummed a tune.

Mistaken

    Simple creatures that they are, they do not grasp the perils of this shining gold. Gather more of it. Take embossed cups from the halls of leaders; chains with layered links like malformed dragonscale; coins by the thousands, such thin, useless bits. Gather all this gold in mounds, like the earth it hails from. It glows in the firelight, shimmers like a brazier but it is a false warmth; this metal feels as chill as death.

    Curl upon the mound — like a guardian beast, a sentinel. Fan your wings to hide the material glow. Noble magicks writhe inside you but they settle, sensing the need for intervention. The gold warms, the mound of it soon reaching the temperature of dragon blood. Outside, the winds speak of pounding feet.

    For soon enough, mankind will recall the existence of these shining trinkets and seek them returned. As though the greedspell sings only for them. As though they hunger and can find no substance to fill their abyssal bellies. Curl on your gold mound and exhale smoke, a grey flag of warning unfurling from the mouth of this cave. Mankind's mortal fear might still persuade them.

It is a benevolent gamble, but a doomed one. The winds speak of nearing feet — in this decade or perhaps the next. The hearts of man are forged in hungry fires, hungrier than yours.

The wind keens a warning and soon the earth speaks, too: raiders talk of a golden hoard. They reach for their crude iron talons. They salivate at the thought of a meal so poisoned. Their greedy bellies keen to be fed.

Watch the cave's mouth and hear the elements cry, hear the anticipation of unbalance. Feel contempt for mankind, and feel pity and sadness strung parallel. Hear the portent of mankind's future sins, these simple beasts entranced by of the ways of war.

The dragon is greed, they say in their yipping tongues. The dragon is desire and cruelty and ruin.

They might someday see their own faces.

Cardiology

Theodore was nearly through with the alpha phase of development. He still reflexively wanted to write a lab report about it. Three hundred and twelve days into the unnamed project, after discarding half a dozen lab coats too soiled to be saved, he was still unwittingly writing introductory paragraphs in his head. Still finding clinical prose drifting like asteroids in his mind.

If he actually wrote those theses down, he would have been at a loss for how to conclude them. He was using gene manipulation in an attempt to make the world a better place. Outlining that wish on hard-ruled lab reports would be like killing joy itself for the autopsy table.

But even if he couldn't articulate his motivations, biotechnology was a tool Theodore was grateful to have. Putting in extra hours of lab work throughout his career had been the best decision he ever made. Even all these never-ending hours of the past year. There was no other use for his time, really.

Pulling a hand through his greasy hair, Theodore tried to stop fidgeting. He was at the end of three hundred and twelve days of mistakes — good ones, bad ones, messes he couldn't begin to classify. He should have found some bravery by now.

He sat at his lab table one final time. The last test Specimen was out of the incubator, a live thing struggling inside its eggshell. The brittle sounds came too slowly, too far apart. Without enough strength to make anything but hairline cracks in the glossy shell. And then the silence held.

Theodore tried to hold his bunched fists in his lap — maintain objectivity, observe without interference — but his Specimen was dying and by everything right, he wouldn't allow that again. With a U-100 syringe near and ready, he took the basketball-sized egg in shaking fingertips. And he pried.

The shell gave way with a crunch and the Specimen spilled out in a tangle of wet limbs — sticky with mucus, its eyes wide, scrabbling with sickle claws like it might grab hold of air to breathe. Theodore put a finger between its jaws — the needle teeth a burning sensation far beyond his hammering pulse — and he slid the syringe down the Specimen's throat, and pulled the plunger. Yellow mucus filled the tube. Then the scrabbling quickened and the teeth sank in whiter, and Theodore pulled the syringe out just as the specimen gargled its distress.

It was suddenly over. Crisis averted. The chimeric hatchling sat calm before him, breathing evenly if hoarsely. Its green scales were drying in the recycled air. Theodore had another dragon.

With his adrenaline burning away, he smiled. And laughed. And wiped his forehead on his grimy coat sleeve and laughed some more, and felt like he might faint onto the table.

"I'm sorry," he told it. "That didn't feel so good, did it?" He still couldn't determine whether the Specimens understood English speech immediately after hatching. They recognized language: that much was clear. Specimen 12 eyed him with flicking slit pupils, inclining its neck the way Theodore now grasped the meaning of. His Twelve was alive and, more than that, it was *thinking*. After so many successes, this still didn't feel old. After so many failures, this was always a miracle.

"You're Twelve," Theodore told it. "That's your name, I mean. And I'm Theodore. And I just need to examine you, to make sure you're alright."

He picked up a pencil and marked down the time of hatching. Liquid sliding over his bitten hand reminded him he was bleeding, and he wiped that on his coat, too. Then he put exploratory hands on Twelve: she quietly allowed it.

This hadn't been the clean unveiling of a perfectly honed mythical creature. This wasn't a glorious dragon from some fantasy realm, however slavishly Theodore had tried. He laid down his pencil — on top of the notes on Twelve's laboured breathing; lopsided skeletal structure; internal rotation of the left hind ankle; crocodilian scutes malformed and grown together in asymmetrical patches.

He pushed all those technicalities out of his mind. Twelve had clear eyes and a well-formed fluid duct in the roof of her mouth. And she was breathing. No one would be euthanized today. Maybe all of them had a chance, Theodore kept hoping.

"You scared me, Twelve," he said, wiping his bleeding hand again. "I thought we'd have to leave without you. I mean, if you didn't hatch, or if something happened."

She placed weight on her clubbed hind foot — and stopped, and craned her neck to stare at the appendage. Like wondering what was wrong with it.

Guilt stuffed tighter into Theodore's chest. He shouldn't have prioritized the mouth duct morphology over such basic functions as walking, but it wasn't as though he had much choice. He wished again for time. And higher-grade food. And fellow researchers, and more extensive DNA banks, and more *time*. Maybe in a hard-won future, his dragons could even have wings like they deserved to.

His enormous wish to succeed was beginning to strangle. Deep breaths, he thought. Stay calm. The Specimens didn't understand all of his words but they knew fear when they saw it.

Removing his glasses, mashing at his eyes, Theodore mumbled, "You'll have wings, Twelve. N-not you, exactly, but your— Your descendants, maybe. They'll make the Lady proud."

By the time he let out a rush of breath and calmed down, Twelve was pawing at his shirt, an excited motion while she stared a plea. Theodore blinked at her.

"Do you know who that is? Lady Almendra?"

Twelve croaked delighted, and her pawing intensified. One claw snagged in the worn cotton. Theodore unhooked that claw and picked Twelve up, gathering her thin limbs into a scaled ball. She was still warm from the incubator yet she pushed, seeking, toward Theodore's mammalian heat.

"Good." He put on his Respectable Member of the Scientific Community Voice. "Specimen Twelve retains memory of prenatal sound stimulus. This seems typical for the species. Well, uh, remembering the Lady is typical for humans, too. She's— She's memorable."

On habit-trained legs, he headed for the Specimens' room.

"We shall know no fear," he quoted for Twelve to hear again. "We shall bow to none."

His own intent dyed those words now. Theodore would never again feel the same as that summer he read the first *Dawning of Shadowkeep* book, curled up on an armchair in the baking daylight. He had stopped merely reading those words: now he going to try following the Shadowkeep principles.

Really go out and try. Theodore couldn't tell whether he was eager or terrified.

Come fair weather, come ribbons of sunlight streaming into her study and setting ablaze the dancing dust in the air, Lady Almendra continued her work. She was an ivory statue at her desk, the rich velvet of her gown a blue cascade down her back and onto the floor. Before her, the fifteen Scrolls of Eternity overlaid one another, their unfurled edges forming a geometry that made their inked letters glow. Lady Almendra changed the Scrolls' arrangement often, noting which letters glowed most vigorous, marking down notes with parchment and ink-dipped quill. The silvery magic lit her fair face — which had long since cast into a pensive frown.

The servant Fadere came to her on care-laid steps, his shabby boots making no noise against the stone. He bore a tray laden with bread, liver paste and pears cut in bone-white wedges.

"My Lady? Please, take this meal. I fear you shall fall ill."

"Fall ill of frustration? I might well." *She sighed and laid her quill down, her slender hand rising to smooth the vexation from her brow.*

"Will you know the spell by the time the stars align, my Lady?"

"I shall. I must. Leave the tray here, Fadere. Gods bless your kind heart. And bring me a flask of elder wine. I shall solve this trial by the dawn — for my kingdom, may it never fall."

When Theodore returned to the Specimens' room, he kicked the door three times. Claws skittered in the room beyond. One of the Specimens grumbled a warning — that was Six, probably shoving the hatchling Twelve out of the door's path.

After a prudent pause, Theodore pushed the handle with his elbow. The box of supplies made a wide blind spot but he smiled anyway, at the glimpse of the Specimens hurrying toward him, squawking greetings and demands.

He had 1.47 kilograms of primate chow for them. That was all the food remaining in this building — all the shelf-stable food still fit for consumption, anyway. Animal kibble always looked plentiful in a bucket, but then Theodore divided it into trays and saw it for the scant kilo-and-a-half it really was. Except for one handful of greasy, brown pellets — which he was hungry enough to covet — he gave his own portion to Twelve.

"This is all we have left," Theodore told them. "Once we go outside, I'll try to find ... I don't know. Stored food, or maybe some escaped livestock. You'll love it. Real meat ..."

The six Specimens gobbled their meal, faces down in their trays. Standing there on four feet and eating kibble, they looked a little like the dogs Theodore distantly remembered in friends' homes. The Specimens resembled dogs in their broadest morphology only, of course. Theodore wondered if lizards would make a more accurate comparison, but he had never actually seen a lizard kept in an ordinary home, eating from a bowl and walking on carpet fibre.

Lizards looked unified, covered in a smooth set of identical scales. The Specimens had no such aesthetic quality, with their manifested patches of crocodile scutes, and curly attempts at feathers growing along their spines, and the jutting, horn-like growths in unpredicted places. And the malformed jaw that forced Six to chew on one side only. And Nine's slurping as he salivated excessively. And Twelve standing there with her club foot held delicately off the ground.

Crouching on dingy lab linoleum, beside the piles of blue surgical scrubs that passed for dragon beds, Theodore tried again to tell himself again that this was an experiment. He was only accomplishing what he could. These results were an incredible scientific achievement: he felt sure of that, forty-nine percent of the time.

Six finished gulping down her half-chewed meal, and came to Theodore with a clicking of claws. She laid her head in his lap; his fingers automatically found her neck and stroked the pebbly-textured skin.

As the trays all emptied, and the last kibble pieces disappeared into mouths, the other Specimens clustered around Theodore. Simply sat with him and offered their various-sized heads for petting. It was a display of empathy for their human caretaker, as well as a borrowing of his metabolically valuable body heat. Twelve climbed into Theodore's lap, between the others Specimens' noses. This was the only sheltered day she would get, and she would probably never know what monotony was.

"We should go," Theodore said to them. "Since you've just eaten. Got to do it while you've got fuel in you ..."

He stood carefully, pushing off the wall while the dragons milled around him. Twelve stayed in Theodore's grasp, curled tight and balanced on his arm.

"Alright, everyone."

Six, Eight, Nine, Ten and Eleven looked to him, their eyes riveted, bodies strung taut with attention.

"Attack procedure."

Immediately, they went to the supply box. Each took a headgear rig in their teeth and, with clumsy but deliberate movements, using forepaws full of non-opposable digits, the five Specimens put on their weapons.

Twelve shifted uneasily. She whined.

"Twelve, you don't need to worry about it," Theodore told her. "You haven't trained to use the headgear yet."

She kept squirming. Wanting to imitate her kin, probably. Sensing the importance. With a grimace meant more for himself than for Twelve, Theodore stepped around the other Specimens and took the last headgear rig from the box. It was too big for her and would need considerable adjustment, but he tightened the rig to her smooth head as much as the jointed arms would allow.

"This headgear will ignite your liquid emission for use as a combustible weapon. So you have, uh. Fire breath." Terms like that still felt strange to speak out loud — like someone around a corner might hear him and raise eyebrows. "I'll teach you to spit later — and the others will show you, too."

There would *be* a later: Theodore could never give up that thought, no matter how improbable.

Twelve simply snapped at the metal arm hovering by her mouth. The other Specimens sat listening, ready to obey.

"We leave in ten minutes," Theodore told them all. "And ... we might not come back. Bring anything we need. Anything we can't leave behind."

The Specimens struggled with the new directive, at first. They picked up empty food trays in their teeth, and the clothing components of their beds; Theodore explained that they could replace those. They picked up the crumpled, claw-torn papers full of Theodore's handwriting, and the archaic portable cassette player that still played its English language learning tape just fine; Theodore found room in his lab coat pockets for those. All of the textbooks had to stay. They were dry subject matter, anyway, good only for gnawing on the hardback covers, and the dragons glanced them over with very little regret.

Eight picked up the only book they all cared about: that old paperback copy of *The Dawning of Shadowkeep, Book 1*. Eight carried the book open, the failing spine bent into an arch, the yellowed pages spread open. Theodore took it from his dragon's mouth and couldn't help looking at the printed words, the ones that pulled at his nostalgic heart.

The dragons circled Lady Almendra, their bowing necks like the archways of her own castle and just as much a home. Her hands brushed over all of their brows, landing finally on the largest-spined brow ridge, that of mighty Skorrnax. Each dragon rumbled its devotion, its love. In all the kingdom, there was no fonder place in that moment than that dragon stable; the piercing wind batted Lady Almenra's skirts around her but it could not drive away her warmth.

"My dragons, my dear ones. Your sire Rukmior shall not join us in this battle, for he flies in the Farbeyond now. We shall also be without our cavalry today. None but we twelve set out to meet the oncoming enemy, and a smaller army the gods have never looked upon. But by everything holy, we shall prevail."

Their rumbling crested. The language of dragons was not made of words but passions, and they now voiced their will to fight.

Skorrnax tipped his great head to jostle Lady Almendra, and her lips drew into a smile even as she stumbled. But it was a brief lapse; the fair sorceress stood regal, her chin high. She drew her dagger, the keen blade secreted in the thigh holster she wore, and it flashed silver as she aimed its point at the sky. Magic pooled golden in its engraved runes as Lady Almendra spoke:

"By the Sages, may their words echo through time. By the Scrolls, may they preserve all rhyme. All goodness, all light, find these allies all sure. By might, by right, let we seven endure!"

Light burst from the dagger's runes, blinding. Magic enveloped all present and in that moment, Almendra knew the totality of truth.

The light was gone as suddenly as it came. Lady Almendra blinked cautiously, and saw glowing spots like candles before her: the eyes of her precious dragons. She laid soft touch on Skorrnax's face and gazed into his eye: there, behind his ink-slash pupil, burned a golden fire. He bore a gift of strength from the Scrolls of Eternity. His breath flowed shining from his mouth, a magical banner drifting on the air.

"Good," Lady Almendra said. "Good, my darlings. We must depart while the spell holds." She holstered her dagger, and resettled her skirts — and in doing that, her own hands snared her attention. They looked like ordinary flesh. Not shining gold from her palms, where her magic germinated. Not marked significant in any way.

"Am I not infused with the spell ...?" Lady Almendra wondered. "Look for sign, Skorrnax."

She met the dragon's gaze, with her purple eyes full of beauty but nothing more. Skorrnax searched the Lady Almendra with his glowing gaze, and he grumbled a sad answer.

"This cannot be," she murmured. "Am I not a vessel of truth? I have fulfilled all the great Tasks, and I have never harboured doubt ..."

The dragons shifted, unease washing through them. Only Skorrnax voiced it, a lilting growl while he touched his soft nose to Almendra's arm.

"Yes. We must go. Sign or no sign, I shall lead you." She accepted Skorrnax's offered foreleg and climbed onto his great

back. The Lady settled her skirts and touched the dagger's shape beneath them, to be sure her weapon was still there. She felt the swirling presence of magic within her but it was caged now by a crushing doubt.

"Aloft, my dragons," she called regardless. "Take flight! We head west, to face oblivion!"

In the quiet reality of the lab, Theodore took the paperback book from Eight's mouth. He snapped the book shut and and tipped it toward him so Twelve could see the cover art. It was a battle scene so familiar that Theodore could sketch it blindfolded if he was any kind of artist, which he wasn't. Punctures dotted the cover: they were toothmarks from dragons, as real as this reality could manage.

"Yeah, we definitely have to bring this," Theodore said, smiling. "I wish I could read you the other books ..." It was lucky enough that Theodore had brought *Book 1* to reread on the day he was trapped. Starting the Specimens in the middle of the series would be a travesty.

Eight just stared at him, his reptile eyes inscrutable as ever. And he nudged Theodore's hand until the book was safely jammed into a lab coat pocket.

Minutes later, Theodore and the Specimens stood in the echoing foyer, at the lab's front doors. The windows were long since boarded over, and thankfully undamaged. The smell of death leaked in from outside — or maybe from the barricaded South Wing, or the bloodstains soaked brown into the walls.

Wherever it came from, the smell unsettled Theodore more than the dragons: they simply arranged themselves in a V that Theodore hadn't taught them. Six, the eldest and strongest, stood at the head of the formation. Possibly an instinctive behaviour, a holdover from the Specimens' avian genetics; Theodore decided that that theory was unlikely, since he hadn't used any migratory species of birds. His dragons were simply intelligent. It was a wonderful, terrifying thing to think while he held the hatchling Twelve, bending around her and touching a cigarette lighter to each Specimen's headgear.

"Now, they move slowly," he explained, "but they're very dangerous. Don't let them get close to you." He paused, until the struggling flame latched onto the ignition arm of Nine's headgear. Flicking the lighter's cheap little wheel and turning to Ten, Theodore added, "The most dangerous part is their highly contagious illness, and you can't catch that because ... Uh, you just don't need to worry about catching it. But be careful, everyone. Protect yourselves, and each other."

Six flexed her claws against the stone floor, her reptilian body tight as a bowstring. She was less restless than the others, more focused on the outside world that only one layer of metal separated her from. All the times Theodore talked about the disaster must have sunk deepest into her mind.

This would be a first and final trial. No margin for error. Theodore had put so much work into it, so much hope and the entirety of his resources. It was important not to try saving the world just yet. Fight only when attacked; focus on finding food and then another comparatively safe place to rest.

Maybe he couldn't go through with this, said a queasiness inside him. He couldn't take his created allies and set them loose in the streets. They could be hurt or killed — or they could contract the virus by some fluke of their patchwork biology. What if they got outnumbered and overwhelmed? What if the headgear pilot lights went out and they couldn't reach Theodore for a relight?

What if Theodore saw a face he recognized?

No. It was well proven that recovery from the virus was statistically impossible. The infected didn't have enough neural tissue left to count on their fingers, never mind remember loved ones. Stop asking questions, Theodore tamped into his mind. The people he saw in the street would all be turned. All of them. Vicious and remorseless and ... well, evil. His only allies stood beside him now, watching him with slit-pupil eyes.

Theodore was a junior genetic engineer with not nearly enough strength or wisdom. In his inner coat pocket, the *Shadowkeep* book weighed.

Despite agony of that blow, Lady Almendra pushed herself from the ground. Her gown was no less regal for its tears, her skin no less flawless for her own blood upon it. Her eyes burned like purple fire as she matched Dark Baron's gaze, as her magic sputtered in her palms.

The dragons abandoned their own battles — turning their backs on the orc masses, accepting mace blows to their hindquarters with scarcely any notice. They gathered all to Lady Almendra, growling kind worries. Their great bulks formed a living shelter, and magic trailed from their mouths like gold pennants. Lady Almendra leaned on Skorrnax's powerful foreleg as she straightened. And over the dragons' growling, she spoke in a winter voice:

"No, Baron. If you seek to seize this kingdom unopposed, you are as foolish as you are wicked. By Luxere's light, I am Lady Almendra and my dragons burn with the fires of truth. We shall know no fear. We shall bow to none."

A light began to shine within her. First under her breastbone, glowing like lantern's fire, then then luminescence spread through her entire body. The light caught Almendra's eye and she held her arms before her, watching the light trickle into her clenched hands.

Skorrnax grunted to her.

"Yes," she breathed, "it must be." Turning her gaze to the Dark Baron — her eyes now burning golden white — Lady Almendra advanced and her dragons parted like ocean water. Magic rose in her palms, too brilliant for eyes to behold, as she said, "This is the end, Baron. We shall cower no more."

Theodore was no royal leader, as he crouched toward his dragons. It was two minutes past the departure time he had set — but he had to give them final orders. His Specimens broke formation to approach him, to inspect the odd stance Theodore had taken, hunched around little Twelve.

"It's going to be dangerous. I'm sorry. Just remember: know no fear, and bow to none."

Six pushed her brow ridges against his hand, a blunt encouragement.

"All of you," he said a little louder, "know no fear. Bow to none. Don't worry about ... k-killing all of them. Just clear a path and I'll look for shelter."

With a commanding snort, Six returned to her formation position. The others followed. Twelve whined but kept still, her heart a drumbeat within her ribcage.

Theodore's dragons weren't big enough to lean on, so he put his free hand on the floor and pushed himself up. He pulled the lab's master keyring from one overstuffed pocket and he unlocked the front door, its turning mechanism a physical memory from far-gone days.

With his fear and adrenaline, Theodore pushed too hard — so that the door swung open and smashed against the outside wall, calamitously loud. Cold wind rushed in, putrid with garbage and burning oil and death.

In the street, dozens of infected humans stopped taking their jerking steps. They turned glittering eyes to Theodore. They opened pit-dark mouths and moaned, and they lurched toward Theodore, a live food source.

His dragons passed him by, snarling, advancing to meet the threat. Six spat first, a plume of bio-accelerant with fire rushing after it. She was no perfect, mythological creature but she was strong, and she might just save this darkened world.

For the first time in years, Theodore stopped being afraid.

Clearsight

They argued again. This time over the number of limbs a simian could reasonably have. It was such disgrace for two dragons to feel anger over this – a simple matter, some trifle that a few thousand turns around the sun would prove or dismiss. In the wake of white-hot emotions, her heart aglow with shame, Konyung thought it wise to spend time away from Drayke. He had broad wings and an expansive will; he did need ample space.

And so Konyung picked up her scrying orb and suspended it in her aura. Undulating her long body like a swimfish, she flew to the opposite side of the continent with her whiskers flowing in the wind currents, with her orb as a glinting pearl towed behind her. Konyung's own winged reptiles soared these skies alongside her; they screeched, a hoarse and inarticulate use of throatvoice. Her gaze pulled toward them – toward their grand wingspans, the dragon-like grace of their necks, the simple efficiency of their webbed tails. Bodies that had evolved broader and lighter than the last time Konyung had looked on them. Pterosaurs, the future had whispered when she asked. These ones would be named pterosaurs. They seemed so promising.

34

But the future had given more answers to Konyung: it had implied that the pterosaurs would not craft their own mantles, that they would not name themselves. That was still an enormity in Konyung's heart, colder than endless deep space. She had made an error, spending half a million years manipulating the pterosaurs' unseen structure. The effort now seemed like spent ashes, a measure weightless when held.

Perhaps, Konyung told herself in the cloud-hung sky, she would work with microbes again. She would reorient herself with the basic principles of life; such meditation would calm her and hone her vision. That seemed like a wisest course.

She approached a valley hillside, finding jagged stone and swaying green fronds. A cave hid there, its air stale but humid enough to offer welcome. Konyung landed, touching the earth as her creatures did. With stalactites leaking in rhythm around her, she decided this to be her sanctuary. Water had never failed to soothe her.

The scrying orb returned to her hands with but a thought, and her will conjured up a new spire for it to rest on. When she hummed —an echo resounding through the dimensions — the orb harmonized with her. Konyung still had her treasure, the truth of Clarity.

In this workspace, she would craft more beginnings. Already she felt more tranquil, a calmer sea after knowing the wind. She coiled around herself in the orb's scant light. She dipped a claw into a biofilm puddled at her feet – and even before the true scrying began, Konyung found this life form familiar: bacteria, the beginning and end of all life. Awareness burned in her: her first argument with Drayke returned to her memory unbidden.

Bacteria are a basic formative step, Drayke had snapped. His mindvoice hung bitter; he kept his back squared to her. *I do not have to like them.*

No, Konyung agreed. *But they hold truths. Don't forget that.*

He turned back to his work, tension tightening his wings closer to his back. Konyung knew the tale his face told: his lips folded back on his pointed teeth, while he held a tree-ape suspended and adjusted its bone density.

Your flighted things – pterosaurs, you said? Those were worthwhile. And perhaps the running reptiles. I ascended from something like those.

She knew.

But if you waste more millions on simple bacteria—

Hold yourself. I am not wasting any more effort than you.

He huffed hot air. *Can bacteria ascend? Can a single cell be self-aware? You would be stupid to argue.*

You do not have to like them, but they are life. Afford them respect, Drayke. Why work at this if you shun life?!

He said nothing more. His attention to this matter was gone, turned pointedly back to the drowsy-eyed ape he held in truth-charged thrall. Konyung could feel the progression of life's evolution, a tingling scent of reality when she inhaled. Her colleague was cultivating this species of ape for size, strength, and the fore-facing eyes he carried on about.

Those things were but details of dragons, Konyung wanted to say. Trivialities. But she had no words Drayke would deign to hear.

Her sharp-toothed friend would work with his simians until this world ceased to breathe, Konyung knew. There was a sheen in his eye this most recent eon. He had a consuming light in his essence, some magnet pull that called him to the cunning

monkeys and their grabbing hands. Riddance to Drayke. A
dragon's power was not so simple as he claimed.

But even as she thought that, Konyung felt regret piercing
her breast. They were above spite, they the dragons, and they
were too rare among the stars to indulge themselves in
pettiness. She needed Drayke. This vast, varied planet needed
Drayke's Strength as much as Konyung's Clarity.

Their arguments had indeed transpired, Konyung admitted
in her heart with her own orb as witness. She was party to the
squabbling; she had given in to pride, as well. They argued only
because they could not yet see which path to take.

In a fair universe, she and Drayke could land on a new
world and know the right species on sight. *Ah,* they would say.
Here it is. They would touch that destined creature with their
truth, and in a mere few generations a new dragon would turn
its face to the light. They the dragons could carry on across the
reaches of space with more shining dignity. This was a fantasy –
but, Konyung's truest self insisted, it was a possible fantasy.

She sat coiled around her heart for three or perhaps four of
this world's months, long enough for her held droplet of biofilm
to dehydrate, die and crumble to dust. Such was the way of
microscopic life: it was fleeting. But the pattering of water on
cave stone calmed Konyung. She was ever grateful for it, the
water's voice that spoke to her scales and her bones. She came
back to awareness and rubbed the biofilm's remains between her
fingerpads; she would save this grainy trace and compare it to
more recent lives. Millions of beings ebbed and flowed inside
this cave alone. There were still untold chances to find a rare
pearl.

That was motivation enough. With truth-laced thoughts, Konyung began suspending biofilms in the open air. Green ooze thinned beyond eyesight until the cells hung in a barely-existing sheet. She made observations and performed dissections, cutting with the harmless blade of her own truthvision, writing her results into the brightness of her memory. Konyung alternated between rapid minutes of work and decades of entranced thought. She manipulated atoms; she fetched more specimens from the slimes around her; she observed life and its similarities. And her small subjects advanced. These bacteria became the pinnacle of their kind, thriving in green masses, capable of restructuring the very air around them. This transformative behaviour was similar to what Konyung herself was doing. She could not resist believing that, in some era to come, her bacteria would only continue to evolve.

But she had not addressed her earlier mistakes. Her bacteria might be wondrous bacteria and still amount to little. They might beget a new breed of pterosaur that would never rise high enough.

After a hesitation, a year's lapse of heartstrength, Konyung grasped her orb and tapped claws on it. A tritone chime rang throughout the cave; the power of her Clarity brought concentration. This was the song of time still to come. She took a droplet of green film and held aloft with a thought.

What will these beings be named, Konyung asked? Her truth thrummed outward through the orb, a sound racing toward the untold future and echoing back.

Blue-green algae, these would be called.

Named by their own design?

No, said the future.

She had learned not to push further when the future said no. She could not simply ask which species would grow enough intellect to bestow names on others. Such prying only ever drained a dragon's strength – and even if Konyung should find an answer she liked, the future would defy any fixed route she pushed it toward. What did Konyung want to know, then? What modicum of all the truth in the universe?

Will these ones survive? She asked, rotating her blue-green algae cells in the air. *Will they live to see the end of this planet?*

Yes, the future said.

Doubt still muddied Konyung's heart. Her algae would live, and that was well and good. But it was scant reward for her trouble. She spent years phrasing another question, considering viewpoints she had not yet proposed to the future. She considered the combined histories of all known dragons, the circumstances they drew their traits from, and the commonalities between they the ascended. It took long enough that the Clarity closed to her; she reawakened the orb's power with a tap of her claws, and she lifted a fresh generation of blue-green algae into the air.

Will these ones survive a cataclysm? Dragons, after all, needed resilience of spirit.

Yes, came the answer.

That was a welcome thought, to be sure. But not every resilient creature had the merits of a dragon. The shadow in Konyung's heart smothered her now, a fear that made her want to gasp deeply for air.

Will the cataclysm come soon?

Her question faded and did not return.

She tried, *Will the cataclysm come within the next million years?*

Yes, the future said.

Now she knew the source of her unease. Konyung was sensing the approach of some menace; she felt a tremor too faint to explain itself yet. Perhaps tectonic movement, or the gathering violence of a volcanic eruption. Reluctantly, she closed her eyes and focused with all her being, with all the truth in her blood. She asked, *Will the cataclysm come in the next thousand years?*

Yes. It would.

And as Konyung held her focus, there was discord in that returning echo. The replying sound parted around a sense of loss, a circle smitten into the earth. A shape like nothingness. Impact and dust.

Konyung stared into this verity, numb, the cave's water droplets drawing silver lines before her. She had seen a glimmering of this world's doom, the extermination of many beings and many possibilities. Maybe the extermination of all things greater than bacteria. There was no time for a dragon's deep thought, not if she had less than one thousand years remaining. She dropped the bacteria into the sludge they came from and she hurried aloft with her orb in tow, surging back across the continent's wind and weather.

Drayke was not in his previous location. Konyung checked all his favoured places, everywhere the sunlight gathered like molten gold. She found him on a thick-grass savannah, with his neck still craned toward a furred ape. He had likely not paused to breathe for years.

Konyung landed by him, her Clarity drifting close. The parting grass crackled and announced her; Drayke gave her a fleeting glance, his slit pupils sharp enough to cut.

You have returned, he intoned.

There was no time to indulge pettiness. She said, *I have brought forgiveness and I think we should share it. But we should not linger over it.*

Drayke still focused on his ape – lengthening the finger bones, Konyung sensed.

She forced her words calm. *Drayke, I know a fear approaching. I have scried it; some cataclysm will arrive within one thousand of this world's years. Have you looked into space this eon?*

Drayke lifted his head, a frown touching his posture. He spoke only the ice-touched shock of a forgotten duty, a feeling too pointed to need words. After setting his ape subject on the ground – to let it flee urgently into trees' cover – he shifted nearer to his Strength orb, to tap it and and let its resonance wash over his eyes. Then Drayke looked to the sky, out past the blue veil of atmospheric reflection. Seconds passed; his breath constricted. He looked at Konyung — truly regarded her and sent a spark of regret between they the two, for the first time in a epoch.

There is a meteor, he said. *Off course and hurtling toward this planet. I believe it is Object Feisen-Eight, but how could this—* He growled in the flesh of his throat. *Another force must have sent it astray, I accounted for—*

How long, Konyung asked; her mindvoice trembled.

By strictest definition, it will indeed be here within the next one thousand years. We have two days. He spat — a snarling outburst of throatvoice that left embers scintillating on the bare earth. *I should have looked. A mere look into space! Simplicity!*

Work had a way of devouring time. They had both indulged in wasting time; they had both been blinded by selfish pride. How foolish dragons could be.

Awash now with pain and compassion, Konyung said, *Focus, Drayke. There is time to use.* A scant measure of time – since two days was barely enough to summon a truthful thought – but time nonetheless.

There will be a new dragon here, he thought fierce. *From this soil, flying in the light of this sun.*

There might be more than one, Konyung agreed. This planet was so rich and so vigorous.

So this world cannot end.

I want more from the future, as I ever do, Konyung said. *But bacteria will live — they will. And we know well that something will rise high enough to bestow names.*

If that Object strikes at its current velocity, I don't believe anything but bacteria will live. He took to the air, wing membranes snapping with each beat. *I am not willing to see this place robbed of its breadth of life.*

Dread held Konyung tight. *What will you do?*

I can lessen the impact.

No! It– Konyung trained her own eyes into space, feeble though they were compared to Drayke's Strength. And she calculated. Tonne-force and aetherjoules, plus a snatched estimate of the meteor's volume: she had never been skilled with mathematicians' cold tools. But she still knew Drayke was too small and far, far too passionate. *That's futility! Could we not deflect it?*

A century ago, we might have. We have no options now.

But you will– Drayke, no!

I will fail this if I attempt it alone? Join me, then. He hovered steady and, for a moment, their eyes met; regret touched his mindvoice, a silver thread of pain and hope. *Help me, friend.*

Always, she thought. But he asked for strength in the form of raw physical power, another tool that Konyung could not call hers. She choked on indecision.

His emotions simmering aloud, he turned away, calling his Strength orb to rest between his hands. Drayke's beating wings carried him upward; those wings were affixed to strong shoulders, as they ever had been. Above the planet, a meteor screamed silently closer. They had discussed this long enough for the sun to set on one day: time now for swift action.

Konyung had to assist his effort. She and Drayke were colleagues sworn to this task, both full of belief. But what if they failed, said her chill fears? Dragons were eternal but their flesh could still rupture, and their hearts could still be crushed within their chests. Without life and truth, their bones would fade and their orbs would fall out of tune, and both would crumble to dust just as the algae did. This world would be alone. After so many mistakes and misgivings, Drayke and Konyung might leave this world fully abandoned.

She rushed aloft, flying to meet Drayke in the air and strike her claws on his Strength. Its vibration washed over her Clarity orb and when she struck that, too, the tones combined, a fuller force tremoring in Konyung's grasp.

Go, she said. *I will follow. If we are lost, I wish there to be a trace left.*

Good, Drayke said. *But be swift.*

He winged onward, out into the airlessness with a glimmer of flame.

In the thin upper strata of the planet's atmosphere, held by aura and wind, Konyung focused on her Clarity's sound one final time. Its Strength-bolstered trichord was an omnipresent roar, a chorus thrumming in her essence and her molecules. The future opened before her. Konyung did not hope for an answering echo this time. She would give a message and pray that the future held it fast. There was no time to focus her truth:

she simply opened her soul, opened her mindmouth and let the future tear words from her spooled intent:

GreatLargeFillingTheSky

FlightFlyingAllPlacesNowAndEternal

BlazeInsideAndFlowLikeRiversBringPeaceAndFightToKeepIt

BearTreasuresGuardHeirs

SpeakInAGrandVoiceBeforeFireAndBruteSlaying

DraykeKonyung
SeeThemClearly
BeStrong

She pulled back against the roaring infinity, narrowing her view until her aura surrounded her once again. The endless sound stopped. She and her Clarity were alone on the edge of space. And though it pained her heart, Konyung faced the blackness and flew higher. The eons ahead would muddy her message but all that mattered was the listener – and there would be listeners. Intelligent, self-aware beings. The future had said as much in every answer. Some creature on this world would advance to understanding, and refine themselves enough to know language and names. That creature would sense dragons as a truth in their living world, some component of life eternal. With enough good fortune, there would be a new dragon ascending – perhaps more than one.

44

A burst of heat cloaked Konyung as she pushed through the atmosphere, and then all was cold and silent. The meteor loomed up ahead; Drayke was a mere passionate speck against it. Konyung bolstered her aura with all the strength and resilience she knew.

Her hands braced on rock — and she hoped for no more fire, never again.

Iron Workings

Jonnan missed his friends, the fellow human voices through the walls at night. He wanted food, the cooked kind with meat in it. And fleetingly, like a whipping flag of guilt, Jonnan hoped his collection of bloodsoda tabs would stay undiscovered. They were useless — but they were his.

He stood in the whipping wind, clinging to straightforward thoughts. This seemed like a mission — a high-priority one. That truth showed clearly even to a barely-trained human boy. They had dispatched without notice; harried-looking Technician dragons had swarmed the steamcabin, their scaly hands assembling and crating a full set of wingsuit components.

Claws clicked on Jonnan's back, barely felt through the copper techplates. His two-dragon crew readied him for flight. He couldn't recall any shared rumours about his Pilot — not when the Commander's name was renowned and dreaded. Jonnan was under the command of Evkolos the many-lauded one. Evkolos the whispered-of. That veteran dragon sat on Jonnan's back, examining the magitech he would soon fasten his claws into. When an eminent Commander brought a raw, young flighthuman on a mission, one of them usually didn't live to tell stories.

Quell the fear, Jonnan told himself. Obey the dragons and he was more likely to see his own bed tonight. He had never been this high up on a cliffside before: the sensation was distant cousin to all the training. Past his boots and far below, there stood a forest of jnekthorn trees, their purple needles winking through the foliage. Wind shoved him: under his sleeksuit, he shivered.

"Main lines are sound," said Commander Evkolos. He clicked upward, his hissing voice nearing Jonnan's ear. "Secondary lines are sound, as well. One minute away is when we launch."

Clawpoints circled the plugs embedded in Jonnan's neck; his hair lifted like scared birds taking wing.

"Noted, sir," said Pilot Olikx. His voice was a softer hiss, like the evenness of a steam engine. Barely felt by Jonnan, he scuttled over the folded wing webs — checking every stitch and bolt and delicate wire. "All things are at par here."

"Approved. Human, you have no excuse for failure."

"Yes, sir," Jonnan said. To speak it was like spitting out a glass marble, some foreign thing he hadn't forged himself.

"The success of this run is imperative," Evkolos said. He sat unshifting; Jonnan knew his scorpion poise without even looking, his silver scales gleaming the very same as his cold eyes. "We have a narrow strike window. Do not fail me."

"Yes, sir."

"Commander," Olikx said, "it would be more optimal if the human knew our objective."

A click of teeth by Jonnan's ear. "The human only needs to fly where I will him to. And you turn the switches you are told to, Olikx."

"I turn switches more promptly when I understand their mechanisms."

"You contradict me?"

"No, my Commander. I advise."

The dragons sat unmoving. Jonnan hoped his wide eyes wouldn't be noticed, and neither would the adrenaline prickling in him. He wanted Olikx to stop drawing ire as much as he wanted to know what the crystals strapped to his chest were charmed to do.

"A concession to you, Pilot," Evkolos snarled. "Human, this day you carry weapons."

Maybe blindflares, said Jonnan's racing mind. Maybe bombs. Hopefully not a kevrbeam: he knew what happened to flying humans when their kevrbeams backfired.

"In place of a warblimp," Evkolos went on, "those damned ponderous things, we attack with the might of surprise. We shall pass over their supply hub and fire the weapon. The Rvenian attack will be devastated before retaliation is possible, and we will save many Lwothendan lives."

Many Lwothendan *dragon* lives.

"Human, do you understand the significance of this?"

"Sir," Jonnan murmured.

"Be sure your blood flows brisk."

"Sir."

"And Pilot, steer true. Give me no further *advisory*."

"Sir," Olikx replied.

The dragons switched positions with a clatter of claws. Commander Evkolos settled in the small of Jonnan's back and strapped in with clattering buckles, before setting his hands into the control ports. Nerves tingled in Jonnan's spine, spreading forward to his heartblood and then outward through his veins. He was gripped by dragon magic, the inescapable power electricity had over an iron-blooded creature. It was the calmest type of terror ever known.

With a brush of scales and more clicking buckles, Olikx settled on Jonnan's neck. He took hold of Jonnan's neck plug and his magic gripped as well, stringing down Jonnan's arms.

The wind pitched, a wavering scream; the jnekthorns stood far below.

"Commencing," Evkolos said. "Flight in twenty seconds."

Magic surged in Jonnan's veins. The flightsuit whirred its unearthly chord as the two lightweight engines geared up, as the electrified wing webs forced Jonnan's arms upward. Wind pushed again at him. The tailwebbing shifted, unfurling as quick as Evkolos's magic could drive it — and Jonnan's goggles slid down over his eyes and ears, with Olikx's knuckles brushing his temple.

"Human," Olikx murmured hard. He left his cold hands under one earmuff, holding it ajar to make room for his snout. "Jonnan is your name, yes? Listen well: humans live near the Rvenian supply hub. Eight hundred are stabled there. We shall not harm them today if you obey me, instead."

Panic lanced hard through him, merely thinking of disobeying Evkolos. But standing on the cliff's edge, not wanting to jump and not wanting to be killed, feeling so very boneless, Jonnan nodded.

Olikx put the goggle strap down, tugging the earmuff into place. His sharp-tipped hand tapped Jonnan's neck twice — nearly like a friendly gesture. Dragons did not touch humans in such a way.

The tailweb stood wide now, pulling with the wind. Electricity evened into a steady crackling, a whirring Jonnan could hear inside his flesh.

"Commencing," Evkolos barked. "*Fly.*"

Jonnan bent at the knees like in the training exercises. He jumped forward with a sickening gravity, the jnekthorn canopies approaching as he pushed off the cliff edge. Arms wide and pulse racing, his webs caught wind and he rose into the sky.

Jonnan was wingless and so were dragons. But bound together, they soared through the screaming wind. Olikx's magic nudged at his neck plug, shifting Jonnan's arms accordingly. In the distance, Rvenia's grey spires towered above the forest. Steam made twirling columns. Blimps drifted. Something small took flight from a sky platform, perhaps another bound human.

We shall not harm them if you obey me instead.

How was Jonnan to obey such a warped order? Humans were thralls to dragons, just simple mammals with convenient chemistry. How could Jonnan comply more than he already was complying?

Commencing, Evkolos said through electricspeech, his voice tinny in Jonnan's mind. *Bomb activation is begun.*

The crystals in Jonnan's frontplate began to vibrate.

Already?! Olikx gripped the neck plug fiercely; he turned, maybe staring sharp at their Commander. *We are still a dozen flenders from the capitol! Your effort is misjudged!*

Silence, pilot. This tactic has been my success before.

Olikx was silent, and he turned back to the oncoming wind. His grasp shifted on the neck plug's copper, unease made incarnate. Whatever he was planning, Jonnan could only hope for success — and as though Olikx heard that remark of the heart, he again patted Jonnan's neck.

52

The silence held taut for a moment longer. The spires crept closer.

Then, a movement on Jonnan's back — Olikx's hands were gone and and a snap rang out, like something breaking. Crackling magic fled into the air. The grip on Jonnan's body tangled like strings.

Mutiny? Evkolos snarled. *You have no honour? Then Hell take you!*

Sparks cracked. Scraping raked up Jonnan's back, the sound of teeth on scales. His dragons sought each other's throats and in their distraction, his engines slowed and his muscles trembled. Jonnan could only watch the treetops rise toward him, his arms and legs locked open against the bulk of the sky.

Take you, instead, Olikx growled. *Honour is not a thing you know. We shall kill no one today, except for you.*

A sudden thrashing, another scuffling. The magic cinched tighter — and Jonnan couldn't breathe now, held in too fierce a grip. His pulse beat erratic in his ears; his vision greyed and, suddenly, returned.

There was only loud wind now. Wind, and humming weapons, and the lightest touch of one dragon on his plated back.

The Commander is no more, Olikx said. *I tore his safety sail; the fall has surely killed him. Obey me now, Jonnan?*

"Yes, sir," he called in his own true voice.

With a hurried tightening of straps, Olikx took command, his electricity gripping Jonnan's being. They still glided without power, the trees near enough that Jonnan could see purple thorns shining like wet knives.

Tcha! The bombs are too far gone for shutdown. I cannot take both roles: Jonnan, you will be pilot. I will drop these bombs. Fold your left foreleg ten degrees on my mark, and I shall power you upward.

"Understood," Jonnan said. He was soaring to his death, likely, but what dizzying elation it was. His gut filled leaden with the relief he hadn't allowed himself to want; the bombs thrummed against his chest. Maybe this could work.

Continuing, Olikx said.

His magic poured forward through Jonnan's being, and the bombs whistled along the edge of Jonnan's hearing. The spires of Rvenia reared tall on the horizon — and warning sirens screamed among them.

Now! Full power!

Now, now, Jonnan thought, spurring himself hotter and letting his every fear and thrill run unchecked. He lowered one shaking arm and banked left — just as their speed jumped and the wind bit at his face, and four blasts roared below as he spiraled higher. Hot surges threw Jonnan off his corkscrew course, tumbling sky over earth.

Level out, Olikx said. *Face the ground; take control.*

He had to control his fall. Like in the exercises. Jonnan saw the horizon reorient and in that instant, he threw both arms wide — like his intermediate trainer had done while calmly standing.

The spinning stopped. Lift held him again. He flew through swaths of yellow, the smoke billowing and blowing from four gouges in the forest below. Those gouges were meant for buildings. They would have killed thousands of dragons Jonnan had never met — and humans too, if Olikx was telling the truth.

Now, view this turnout! Olikx laughed, a sound like a kettle boiling. *I was told we had a spirited flighthuman. I'm delighted such was so.*

He smiled and wanted to weep instead.

They returned to the cliff face moments later, circling gradual until the lift was gone from under Jonnan, until he fell the final few meters and landed in a crouch that jarred as badly as everyone said. He stayed there while his webs powered down, hunched, anticipating.

Olikx relieved himself of the command seat. He clicked back onto Jonnan's shoulders, speaking with his tongue. "Human Jonnan? Let it be known to you that Renegade Olikx, formerly of Lwothendan's Aviary, has stolen you this day." He paused. "You may be freed if you wish it. Admittedly, I am not sure where an unbonded human might go from here."

Jonnan didn't know, either. He had never eaten a meal not served to him in dragon-wrought metalware. He knew stories of human tribes living proud and free in ancient times but he had no inkling how they had done it. With questions on his tongue, he bowed his head. All he knew was how to be a flighthuman.

"You're a Renegade," he asked Olikx, quiet and bold. "What is that?"

"It's a new effort! Renegades are we who snarl in the face of war. Truly, now, it's senseless that dragonkind claims to value honour, then we force lesser beings to aid us in killing by surprise. But in honesty …" Olikx paused again, and tapped his claws rhythmically on the flightsuit. "I did not consider what to do with you after the mission was thwarted. This is my error. Really, how am I any better by forcing you to comply with my mutiny?"

Muscles wearying now, Jonnan shifted and sat on the wind-scoured rock, slumping with the weight of all this. He wished to see Olikx, not just hear him. Dragons didn't paint their emotions across soft mammal faces but they did show certain shades of mood in their positioning, in the way they held their horned heads.

"Well," Jonnan ventured, "your end justified your means, didn't it?"

Olikx hummed. "End justifying my means ... Vraa, what an artful phrase."

"It's nothing ... Humans say it a lot."

"Never where dragons can hear it, I presume."

Jonnan hummed negative.

Quiet held, in this bubble of peace surrounded by wind. The forest waved below, thorns obscured by humble leaves.

"You will need food in a few hours," Olikx mused.

"I'd like it sooner than that. I-if it's possible."

"Truly? Ah. Well, Jonnan, I declare myself your field owner. I shall now take you to Wrenios, with your concession of help. Facilities are in place there for the wardship of humans without owners. The owners of such facilities are allies of the Renegades — perhaps they can find a civilian home more permanently suitable for you."

Even if they couldn't, said a tentative newness in Jonnan's heart, he might not mind. He had never liked a dragon before — but Olikx stood for something, a principle other than blind pride.

"That sounds fine," Jonnan said. "I'll follow your commands, sir."

"Excellent!" Claws scrabbled as Jonan's one dragon returned to the command seat. "Are you ready to fly, Jonnan?"

"I'm not used to being asked whether I'm ready for things," he admitted. He got to his feet.

Laughing again, Olikx said, "What foolishness it is, not to ask! Chaa! Commanding you to be ready when you may not be capable of such a thing. This is a nonsense I've spat on since I joined the Aviary — though, not in words. Or in literal spitting."

Olikx was not a renowned dragon. He didn't speak dissent where ears might hear him, because that was the only cautious thing to do. Lower-ranked dragons were nearly like humans, Jonnan now dared to think.

"I'll ask again. Are you ready to fly?"

"I think so." Stepping again to the cliff's edge, Jonnan felt a smaller measure of fear as he looked down at the distant jnekthorns. Dragon magic surged hot in him, and he raised his wing-webbed arms.

On his second real flight, Jonnan flew westward on webs he moved himself. He would never see his soda tab collection again, and he carried a tentative friend. It felt nearly like freedom.

Another Odyssey

Morning peels the sky apart. Awareness cleaves the dragon's mind and she stirs. She goes to the back of the house and opens the screen door with a squeal of hinges — so that the day greets her, warm summer against her scales. A new day. Her roar reaches the heavens.

The phone rings: the neighbours express once again that they dislike the roaring.

But she is proud and unfettered, and she only snarls a little while setting the coffee maker. It vexes her as always, its beetle-small buttons defying her claws. But she brings it to life. The dragon sits over the steam-spouting device, its every drip a gathering treasure.

Realization spears her. She turns to the refrigerator, circling her bulk tight so her tail spines slide harmless over the cupboard doors. She opens the fridge and lo, a cold empty space meets her where the creamer ought to be.

The dragon growls. She hungers for a cow, a groaning, kicking piece of prey to sink her teeth into and, at some point before or afterward, get a little cream from. But she has fielded one phone call today — *already* — and the local farmers are troublesome when crossed.

She walks out into the summer light, screen door banging behind her. Wings unfurled, she takes to the sky, soaring free and also taking a crumb of delight in how her wingbeats bend the neighbours' lilacs, the accursed things that are no use for eating.

The supermarket sprawls below her like a grey mud flat, its parking lot not yet livid with the day's heat. The dragon lands, mindful of her claws: cars hunker all around and they are dangerous yet fragile.

Flat human faces turn to her as she enters. The dragon stoops to pass through the door and then lifts her head magnificent, a vision of might as she chooses a plastic basket. One forepaw bent delicate around the basket's handle, she walks past the stands of tropical fruits and leafy cow-food, her gait uneven but proud. The treasure she seeks lies farther inside.

Cold hangs ominous in the dairy aisle, the combined breath of a dozen silver refrigerator units. The dragon sits before one and rakes it with her eyes, and she snarls annoyed. Her brand is absent. Another cold, empty space meets her.

And so she stands considering the other milk cartons, those less desirable. Cold sinks its fangs through her scales; she despises it. She focuses on the many pictures and percentages behind the condensation-silvered glass.

Beside her, a human speaks its nasal, reedy tongue. Has the dragon tried those flavoured creamers? The pumpkin spice one is delicious!

The dragon snorts steam. The refrigerator door is fully white now, too marred to see through.

The human has been trying all the flavours, he shrieks. Figures he might as well treat himself in the morning! The pumpkin spice one is really good, though. The dragon should try it.

She yanks the door open and takes a carton that plies beneath her claws, full of a fat percentage she no longer cares about. She cannot leave the dairy aisle fast enough.

The cashier — a young, female human with plastic baubles in her hair — is unfamiliar with the gold coins of a dragon's hoard. She turns the coin over and back again. She asks if it is real money.

The dragon growls.

Does the dragon have any other form of payment, the cashier asks? Maybe a credit card?

She misses the days when humans fled screaming before her.

After dealing with a rotund management human, she returns home. Uproots a damnable lilac bush with an intentionally misplaced claw, and slams the door behind her, and puts the creamer on the countertop in its slightly crushed carton. The dragon turns to her coffee maker. The contents remain hot, though they smell bitter as the ashes of a razed village. She will need a common trove of this human epoch: sugar.

62

She curls taloned fingers around the glass sugar shaker. She looks at it, and she snorts. Empty as well, this one. Devoid of the sugar she could have obtained from the store full of groceries — but she did not.

Hurling the screen door open, bellowing her ire, the dragon storms outside into the day. She takes flight. She hungers for a cow, so she will have one — and fates help the farmer who defies her.

In Lifetimes Spared

Queen Lumina arrived to find the dragon awaiting her. Vivekr the Terrible laid beside the new building, coiled there like a mountain of golden scales and sailcloth wings — and he watched the approaching humans with narrowed eyes.

Lumina reined her horse to a halt. The Holy Regiment stopped behind her with a clamouring of hooves and ring mail.

"All at ease," she called. "Hail, Vivekr. A shining welcome to you."

He huffed, smoke jetting black from his nostrils. It hung coiling on the grass while Vivekr raised his many-horned head.

Movement rustled behind Lumina: the easing of many hands toward polearms.

"Bright day to you," Vivekr replied. His sonorous voice only growled slightly while speaking a human greeting.

Queen Lumina stepped down from her mount's back, into an assistant's laced hands, and onto the sparse grass. She wore a new riding tunic — cut long in the back to resemble a proper gown, embroidered as finely as any silk. From around her neck, she unlatched the pendant phial of blessed water. She approached the new hall on sure strides and paid no mind to the dragon's gaze upon her.

She tipped one drop of the blessed water onto the earth, as near to the hall's foundation as she could manage. It soaked in dark while Lumina murmured the ceremonial words in the ancient tongue. She touched the crown nested in her grey-streaked hair. And with that, the hall was committed to her queendom, a new addition that would serve all righteous folk.

"It is done," she announced. She turned to regard her Holy Regiment.

They were four dozen sturdy men and women, sitting astride war horses, armed and ready. They wore the grim faces of soldiers not sure whether there would be war, and uncertain whether to hope for it.

"Holy Regiment. Forget not your orders."

Keep a keen-eyed watch and nothing more, she had told them, firm. *Do not engage Vivekr. Make absolutely no threat upon the dragon, for this day he is an honoured guest. Whatever orders you received from Princess Solani, discard them: your Queen speaks now.*

They answered Lumina with the ringing of gauntlet knuckles against polearm blades.

Beside the Holy Regiment were the cookstaff, unloading sacks from ox-drawn carts, unsure where to set their saucer-wide eyes.

In a softer voice, Lumina told them, "Begin preparations. Walk with ease. Vivekr the Terrible has no reason to harm you."

She felt the dragon's attention behind her. Maybe a toothy grin, depending on his mood.

Lumina's assistants hurried to the great hall's doors, gliding like spirits in their white cloaks, and they grasped the handle rings. They bent against the door's weight. Greased hinges keened. Slowly, the entrance yawned open and the cooks hurried through it with burdens held.

Lumina extended a gloved hand. "After you, Vivekr. I insist."

Once on his feet, he was a hundred feet of sinuous beast, a primal force with sunlight banding along his golden scales as he walked past. With dagger teeth bared — teeth full of a most potent venom — he hissed his dragon's laughter. "Too gracious, Lumina."

Sometimes, she wondered if she was.

It was commonly held belief that a dragon smashed and devoured anything in its path, heeding no hunger but the wish to destroy. Lumina knew better. She had seen the inside of Vivekr's cave too many times to be ignorant; despite her girlish screaming, she managed to see the surprising array of fragile treasures owned by a supposed monster. He had a teapot, a jewel-crusted one stolen from a noble in some far-gone century. That teapot — after many times regarding it — inspired Lumina.

The cooks worked with stifled commotion, building fires and readying trays for the heat. The kitchen boy brought kettle after kettle to fill the steel-banded teapot appropriately sized for a dragon. They would drink tea infused with redwort today, as Vivekr had discovered he liked.

Vivekr sat on his haunches at the table, a hewn slab of granite polished until it shone like a gem. He poised his neck as a proud swan would, and he cast a discerning eye over the hall — the split marble walls with girders carved from giant bone; the oceanwraith scales layered like shingles to make a shimmering, silvery ceiling; and the cavernously large fireplace, lined inside with obsidian and piled high with blazing, crackling pine boughs.

"Do you like the craftsmanship of this place, Vivekr," Lumina asked. She poured tea from an ordinary porcelain teapot, and the scent of redwort lapped like waves against her memory.

Vivekr snorted. "It's boxy. The materials are clever, though. I thought humans made dwellings from treewood."

"Sometimes."

"When circumstances demand it, I suppose?" Vivekr reached for his teapot, savouring its shape under his heat-resistant pawpads. "Kah."

"When a giant cannot easily be felled, yes," Lumina said lightly. She stirred cream into her tea, a white spiral vanishing. "This building, however, was made for the very purpose of our meeting."

He inclined his head. That sentiment lodged in his primal heart, Lumina knew: he liked value in all its forms, even the sentimental sorts of value that could not be held in greedy hands.

"Your subjects agreed to it?"

"I used my personal funds." Lumina paused, pressing her lips. "I do not know the precise feelings of the labourers who raised these walls. I do know, however, that the engineer approves of such concord."

Vivekr inclined his head, scrutinizing this Lumina, this Queen. In the dark pools of his eyes, his silver pupils darted like fish.

"Your garments are new, as well," he commented. "They become you more than the puffy things."

She lifted a hand to the tunic's collar, rubbing the needlework between thumb and forefinger. "Yes. As a matter of fact, the pearl buttons come from the Yilsevar Coast. They provided our meal on the last occasion we met — the sailfin fish, and all the oysters. The Yilsevar Coast is in favour of concord with dragons; their support is nearly unanimous as of the last public query."

Stirring pepper into his oversized teacup — with a silver spoon the size of a shovel, gripped in a fisted forepaw—Vivekr growled a considering note.

"Eight of the twelve regions are in concord," Lumina added. "If I passed a decree today, the councils would not oppose me."

Quiet hung. The cooks brought trays mounded with steaming, fragrant meats.

"I will not ask the other dragons," Vivekr decided. "Not this day, nor a thousand of your piddling human lifetimes from now."

"Vivekr," she sighed.

"No." His dark eyes narrowed. "You are aware of whom you speak with, princess."

The assistants stiffened beside her. Lumina held a political expression but truly, she didn't mind the nickname. She considered the dull red contents of her teacup — which she held in withering hands, covered with satin gloves.

<u>I do not even like humans,</u> Vivekr told her once, snarled in a most menacing tone.

Princess Lumina, with her crushed dress hoops, rumpled hair and stricken dignity, had nearly believed him. Vivekr the Terrible was a dreadful beast who had snatched her away to a dirty cave. He deserved blades through his heart, the Princess had vehemently thought.

Queen Lumina sipped her tea, feeling the weight of her own bones. She set the cup down. "Pride forbids you from asking your fellow dragons, I suppose?"

Craning back, Vivekr held his head high like his horns were a great many crowns. "Pride is first and foremost! Who ever heard of an Ancient One sharing food with a mere human? Breaking bread, I imagine you would say. Bread!" He picked up a dumpling from the edge of a meat platter. "What is this? A paste of wheat flour?"

"I wouldn't offend you so," Lumina said mildly. "They're potato dumplings. A common food for labourers and other humans who live by their strength. They do not typically contain meat but for this honoured guest, I had the cooks add chopped loin of venison and shape the dumplings large."

Vivekr held her gaze. Then he reconsidered the lump of food between his clawpoints. He put the dumpling in his great maw, and chewed grudgingly as though he might be bitten back.

Lumina said, "If Vivekr the Terrible, the dragon of possession, can find common footing with a mere human, then why not the others?"

"Common footing! As though we travel on two muddy feet!"

Lumina stifled her sigh, and instead picked up a serving fork to take some spiced mutton.

"I cannot even ask Revntka the Mighty," Vivekr continued, "not until she resurrects. Ziorknor might consider the matter, but only if humans were an owned thing to steal from me. Are they?"

"Hardly."

Vivekr huffed, veiling the table with smoke. He took a thick slice of roc meat together with a dumpling, and chewed them while he went on: "Revntka's resurrection! Let us not forget such indignity, that dragons are slain by upstart humans. Why should we wait half a year to return to life, only to crawl on our bellies once we arrive?"

"I recall no crawling from Vivekr the Terrible. And I name you as my honoured guest, do I not? Just as I was a guest to you."

His dagger smile emerged, slow but inevitable. "Time erodes your mind, princess. You were no such thing as a guest."

She picked up her teacup, enjoying the tea's smell more than its flavour. "I'm quite aware of time, actually. Today is the anniversary of Sir Gavelling's death."

Vivekr straightened. The dragon towering over her suddenly looked small, a wide-eyed whelp within his own body. "Gavelling is dead?"

"One year ago today, yes."

Vivekr's eyes darted, searching the air and finding nothing.

He must have heard the same echo Lumina did, the distant shout of Sir Gavelling at the cave's mouth:

Ho, vile worm! I am Sir Gavelling of the Isle, sworn to all that is right. By God's grace, I shall save Princess Lumina!

Those words stirred Lumina's heart — that first time when she was terrified, and even the tenth time when she knew what to expect. That shout still touched her in a place of fondness, a place now grey with time and regret. Sir Gavelling was a most noble lendlance, and the cleverest fighter still bound by fair play. The likes of him were spoken of in ballads and rarely seen in flesh.

"I shall speak one praise for humans," Vivekr decided. "You are creatures of precise timekeeping. Is it one year exactly?"

"It is, indeed. What is the hour," Lumina asked the assistant removing her cold teacup.

"Sixteenth hour and twenty minutes, Your Grace."

"It is one year today, very nearly to the minute."

Vivekr stared, his eyes black oceans with minnows lost in them. "He died in combat ...?"

"I regret to say that he did not. After slaying you the last time, Sir Gavelling swore that his next noble deed would be to destroy the ogre of Bentroot Mire. Not one more child would be eaten, he declared. He fulfilled that oath, but before it died, the ogre crushed his bones from without. He passed away in a sickbed."

"Gavelling was my—" Vivekr lashed his tail. "He was a passable warrior. He sired Princess Solani, did he not?"

"No. He might have been my husband, though."

Brave, kind Gavelling should have been king, said that distant place in Lumina's heart — but she dared not utter such a truth.

"And," Lumina ventured, "I think he would have liked to see humanity and dragons make concord."

"Fah! He wanted dragons dead, and to stay that way."

"He didn't! It's truth." Lumina took another portion of the well-seasoned mutton. "Gavelling ... He only really wanted an end to the battle and conquest. He thought no one ought to live fearful of what was to come. No one should be snatched up by bloodthirsty beasts. Some called him foolish ... But I have never known those opposers to take up a lance themselves."

Vivekr thought on that. He poured more tea, and Lumina cut and ate her meat. The sun hung incandescent outside the hall's window, the afternoon fully present. Vivekr clutched his cup and watched a cook removing empty platters — and his attention came so sudden that the girl flinched like she had been doused with water. He then returned his consideration to the fine porcelain bedecking the table. His own plate was large enough to hold an entire banquet of food, if humans were to eat it.

"For all his bold words," Vivekr said, "Gavelling was not a hateful man, was he?"

"I've never known one kinder. I asked him once, if he wished upon starlight and he might have anything, what would he have?"

Lumina was still a girl when she had asked that, and a vain girl besides. She had been hoping for a compliment from the brave man peering out of the armour. Some gilded prose about a woman of his dreams. His modest answer had left a bitterness in Lumina's mouth — and she didn't acquire a taste for bitterness until much later in her life.

Lumina was a girl, then. Still curling her hair each morning, and painting her cheeks, and going about with her smooth hands ungloved. Still seeing each day as a trinket to be discarded.

She smiled tight and wry now, surely drawing more lines into her own flesh. And she told Vivekr, "Gavelling said if he could have anything God might grant, he would wish for peace."

"Peace ...?!"

"For every living thing, that we might all somehow live shoulder to shoulder." She laughed, a lightly falling sound. "Can you imagine?"

Vivekr snorted smoke. "So he didn't even *wish* to die in battle."

"Vivekr."

"Well, why do you suppose dragons have endless appetites, princess? Why do we fight the lendlances that come bawling to our homes, when we could simply fly away and let our stolen maidens be taken back? To desire something and then simply stop — that's as good as failure. One should want life as powerfully as a fire wants fuel." He peered at her from under ridged brows. "That's no wisdom for humans, though. You're short-lived things ... You only end up dying for good."

Putting her fork down, Lumina understood a little more. She said, "Gavelling still would have liked to see us dining together, though ... By invitation and not by force."

The dragon rumbled, one note of agreement. His gaze skipped across the various tableware.

"And I still hope that my daughter will join us for a meal. I've explained that the years change one's mind about dragons. But I think Princess Solani needs to speak with you before she can have any measure of faith."

Vivekr shifted on his haunches, like the sentiments were cooking him within his scale armour.

"We need not plan that meeting today. I would only like you to consider it."

He picked up his plate with careful paws. "Hold this plate for me, if you would, Lumina. I have noplace safe enough to store such a fragile thing."

Lumina agreed. His tastes had shifted away from fragile things, these past decades. He coveted wealth as much as ever — but he had no more stomach for loss.

The assistants doused the hearth fire; the cooks packed their roasting pans and seasonings. The head cook mustered enough courage to ask Vivekr if the meal suited his tastes — and the dragon surprised Lumina with his civility:

"It was well made," Vivekr said, regarding the cook with the corner of his eye. "But use a stronger hand with the garlic next time I am a guest."

They were late enough leaving as it was; afternoon lay heavy in the sky, and their journey back would last well into the night. Lumina climbed onto her horse, arranged her tunic's tails and turned a smile to Vivekr — who sat fifty yards away, the nearest a calm horse would tolerate.

"I must thank you again for attending, good Vivekr," Lumina told him. "And I do hope that concord between our kinds might happen in my lifetime."

"That's a truly shining ambition you have," he said, dry as parchment. "But ... this was a fine idea. This hall of yours."

"A shining farewell, Vivekr." She lifted the reins.

"Queen Lumina."

The dragon never called her that. Her blood touched with frost, Lumina turned back to him — and found Vivekr staring away at the distant mountains.

"Be cautious on your journey home," he said. Then he rose and departed, walking and then winging away more promptly than he did anything.

Lumina ordered the Holy Regiment into defensive formation: a dozen soldiers before her, a dozen behind her, and a dozen at each side. They travelled in such a way, steady through the patchwork pine forests. Lumina watched the tunic-clothed backs of her personal guard, and their many faces sweeping the surroundings. Alongside Lumina, the Holy General guided his horse closer.

"Your Grace, do you know what the dragon meant?"

"He has never spoken in riddles to me before."

Dragons were magical creatures but not cryptic ones: that was Lumina's impression, based mainly on her time spent in

Vivekr's cave, watching him mellow toward his human prize. Lumina wanted to turn her eyes downward, girlishly — and she did no such thing in front of her guard.

"If Vivekr is willing to discard his pride and speak a warning to us," she said, "we would do well to heed it. And he was vehement about not trusting his fellow dragons ... Expect an attack from the sky, if at all."

Around her, guards turned their faces upward.

The General nodded, crisp and obedient. "We received word this morning that Urnveos the Fitful is heading north. Her chaos knows no pattern — and yet, it does. If she is the threat Vivekr speaks of, we will be able to sight her well in advance: Urnveos has a distinctive flight cadence and her thunderbreath is visible from leagues away."

Lumina pressed her mouth. "I would not wish to battle Urnveos. Nor any dragon. But if we do sight a dragon on wing, tell me, General: what would this regiment—"

A shout from one left-flank guard was all the warning they had: the trees ripped aside from a great green wedge of a lunging beast. It was Ziorknor the Fierce. The shouting guard was silenced, snapped up in Ziorknor's razor teeth while his horse thrashed and shrieked. All around Lumina was a sea of panicked horseflesh and guards drawing polearms, while the dragon shook a human warrior with long snaps of his serpentine neck.

"Holy Regiment!" bellowed the General, "We shall never surrender the queen! Use fire precautions!"

Ziorknor threw the limp soldier aside with a toss of his head, and he stood crouched on four feet, hissing a blood-mouthed laugh. "So clever, you small men!"

Lumina was off her bucking horse, held by her assistants' fear-firm hands as they scrambled backward together. She saw in glass clarity the moment Ziorknor sucked in a breath, his webbed fins pressing tight to his neck, and then his torrent of emerald fire. Men and women screamed; ward spells sang a quavering note against the flames.

"Ziorknor," Lumina shouted, her voice reedy in the midst of chaos, "take what you will! Our possessions are better off as yours!"

The dragon of jealousy turned yellow eyes to her, sharp as scythes; he knocked three guards away from his underbelly with a flick of his forepaw. "Well met, queenling. I want your life."

Four guards charged toward Lumina and turned their backs to her; they raised four polearms, blades pressed together in twin peaks. One of them chanted in a panic-sharp voice — and an assistant at Lumina's right side joined in, echoing the ancient words that bound a ward spell onto the polearms' metal. The glassy wall of magic rose and an instant later, the tide of green fire struck it, a smothering heat pouring around and past.

Over the sound of straining magic, a roar tore the sky — a familiar one that made Lumina's heart leap hopeful. Vivekr voiced a challenge. On spread golden wings, he fell onto Ziorknor, and Lumina knew a most awful joy as Ziorknor snarled. With the Holy Regiment guards scrambling away, the two dragons tumbled and clawed, broke free of each other and stared with white-hot spite.

"How shameful, Ziorknor," Vivekr snarled, his teeth all bared and his black venom dripping from them. "Trying to take my humans from behind my flank."

"Less shameful than your mockery! Holding a gathering of insects so near to my domain!"

The hall was built three leagues distant from Ziorknor's territory. Lumina recalled the silver pin in her map, and the inked line an inch away — but Ziorknor was the dragon of jealousy, and not a creature fond of reason.

"Near to your land," Vivekr said, "but still within mine. You shall not have what's *mine*." He lunged, his open jaws seeking.

Ziorknor was the larger dragon and the more sturdily built — but with Vivekr at his throat, he staggered into the yielding trees. "You still desire her? I thought you had given up. You don't so much as steal her anymore."

The Holy Regiment regrouped, clustering together before Lumina to form a human wall. She watched between their shoulders and through two layers of ward spells — as gold and green struggled; as wings beat futilely; as venom and fire sizzled against dragon scales. She had never trembled so fearfully in all her life.

It all faded into quiet. Vivekr's growling was muffled, his jaws a vice around Ziorknor's throat.

"You fool," Ziorknor wheezed, nothing left but his bitterness. "How dare y—"

There was a final sound — like a sword wedging under a dragon's scales. But this wasn't Gavelling's sound of triumph. This was the slower, fleshier tearing of dragon claws.

It was over. Ziorknor the Fierce fell to earth like so much sackcloth. With glances to one another and to their General, the Holy Regiment allowed their ward spells to fade.

And Vivekr shifted on his feet, looking away from the great, green corpse and back again. He dug his bloodied claws into the cleansing earth with a sudden passion of movement. A dragon had never killed one of its own kind, not in all the tomes of history. Squabbled with fellows, plenty often, and scarred them — but never killed. Vivekr must have known that truth like cold iron embedded in his heart.

Lumina stood there, a queen but still one small human. She touched her pendant phial and found it blessedly present. She smoothed escaping hair back against her head, and brushed mud from her crown before replacing it on her head. Then she rose, and under the many stares of her entourage, she approached the dragon on quiet footsteps.

Vivekr ceased clawing at the earth. He spat an inky clump of venom into the hole and stood breathing raggedly over it.

"I might have been killed if you hadn't arrived," Lumina told him. "Even if I escaped harm, we would have lost many more soldiers. Thank you, Vivekr."

"I shall have no end of trouble when Ziorknor resurrects." He ground his teeth together. There was more he didn't say: Vivekr the Terrible was far too proud for it.

"Among humans," she said, "it is considered a great and noble deed to protect a member of royalty."

"I know that," Vivekr spat. "I knew Sir Gavelling."

"Well ... If you should ever find it acceptable to visit the Capitol, there shall be a ceremony for you, and a medal of valour. Engraved finely. Made of gold and lazuli." Vivekr would love a valour medal with all his covetous heart, Lumina realized.

"Visit the Capitol," he hissed, laughing. "As though I could land there and be welcomed. You're still too gracious, Lumina."

With his golden head bowed, he looked not like a beast at all.

An introduction to the Stories of Aligare

The following two stories are set in the Aligare world, among people who are not humans. The three peoplekinds live together in varied mixtures, with no history of war or racial strife. They collaborate and still have troubles to face.

Aemet   Ferrin   Korvi

In this world, tales of family and friendship begin.

82

The Korvi's Limbs

In the land of Aligare, the three peoplekinds share their wisdom by telling legends. A legend might be passed down through the generations, or simply made up on the spot — either way, they are a cherished form of education. This is one such legend.

Long ago, when the land was new and the first plants pushed leaves toward the light, the gods chose their peoplekinds. Great Fyrian, god of fire, chose the korvi as his children because they blazed within their hearts. Fyrian granted them firecasting magic so they might shed warmth wherever they went.

In that time so many generations ago, the korvi were far different. They were not dragonkind yet — only a simplest form of lizardkind. They had no arms, no legs, no wings on their backs and no horns topping their heads. Korvi crawled the earth alongside many other snakes — but unlike snakes, the korvi often paused in their crawling and turned their faces toward the sky.

Great Fyrian landed on hot Volcano rocks one day. He saw a korvi twisting its long body off the ground, gazing wistful at the sky full of clouds.

"Hello, child," Fyrian said. "What is it you seek?"

"Great One," the korvi said, "I long for the sky. I am close to the warmth of your firerock within the earth and I am grateful, but there must be more for me."

As Fyrian looked upon his child, he saw a spark inside. A spark that would begin a fire, if it were given tinder. But no one could simply give a creature new fate, not even a god.

"Very well," Fyrian said. "If you can bring me something that has touched the sky, I shall give you arms."

The korvi agreed to this wager and slithered quickly away.

That korvi searched all over the mountainside. There were many rocks and stones and patches of sand — all of which touched the air, but not the splendid sky's heights where light showed its colours. If the korvi was bound to the earth, he wondered, how could he reach something that had touched sky?

After much wandering, the korvi came to the base of the Volcano where lowland soil gathered. And here, the korvi found a polegrass plant. It stretched tall above him, waving a heavy seedhead. The korvi pushed at the polegrass's stem and it bent, lower and lower until the korvi could grab that seedhead in his teeth. He hurried back to the mountaintop, where Fyrian waited. He laid the seedhead before his god.

"This has touched the sky, Great One," the korvi said. "It grew many times higher than I can reach." The korvi's inner fire burned brighter now, fed by ambition.

Fyrian saw this and he was pleased. He gave the korvi a gift of arms, and for the rest of his days that korvi roamed the mountainside giving arms to every fellow he met. Korvi folk still looked to the sky, but they did it straight-backed, bearing limbs and a kindling sense of pride.

A generation passed. Then Fyrian landed on warm Volcano rock, and he saw another korvi. Sitting with her long body poised off the ground, gazing wistful at the sky full of clouds.

"Hello, child," Fyrian said, "What is it you seek?"

"Great One," the korvi said. "I long for the sky. These arms let me reach upward and I am grateful, but there must be more for me."

Fyrian looked upon this child and saw a fire inside. A steady fire that would burn brighter, if given the fuel.

"Very well," Fyrian said. "If you can bring me something that has touched more sky than the polegrass, I shall give you legs."

The korvi agreed to this wager and slithered quickly away.

That korvi searched all over the mountainside, and farther into the lowland forests. Trees threw shadows over her and the korvi stoked her fire hot against the chill. But although most of the trees' leaves grew in shadow, the topmost leaves were bathed in light. With her hands and tail, the korvi gripped cracks in the tree bark and she climbed, higher and higher until she could grab a topmost leaf in her jaws. She hurried back to the mountaintop, where Fyrian waited. She laid the leaf before her god.

"This has touched the sky, Great One," the korvi said. "I climbed far from the ground to reach it."

Fyrian saw this and he was pleased. The korvi's inner fire burned hotter, as lively as a festival song. He gave the korvi a gift of legs, and for the rest of her days that korvi ran over the the mountain and through the forest, giving legs to every fellow she met. Korvi folk stood tall now, holding their bodies well off the ground and watching the sky always.

A generation passed. Then Fyrian landed on hot Volcano rocks and he saw another korvi. Standing as tall and straight-backed as he could, head held high as he looked up at the sky.

"Hello child," Fyrian said. "What is it you seek?"

"Great One," the korvi said. "I long for the sky. I stand tall enough to feel the wind on my hide and I am grateful, but there must be more for me."

Fyrian looked upon his child and saw flames. Flames that could heat the broadest corners of sky, if given the means.

"Very well," Fyrian said. "If you can bring me something that has touched more sky than a tree's leaves, I shall give you wings."

The korvi agreed to this wager and loped quickly away.

He searched all over the mountainside, and farther into the lowland forests, and deep into the oak glades that ferrin and aemet people called home. The korvi met these otherkind folk and asked them how to climb up to the skies over their treetops. But with sad faces, ferrinkind and aemetkind told him they didn't know how to reach the sky. No peoplekind did.

The korvi didn't know, either, but he was too full of fire to be dissuaded. He found the tallest oak in the land and scaled it with his clawed hands and feet. At the top of this tree, the korvi turned his face up toward the clouds wafting in the golden sky. And with his hands outstretched, he jumped toward them.

The fall was terribly painful. But lying on the leaf-blanketed earth, the korvi found beads of water in his hands, grabbed from water god Okeos's gathering rain. The korvi limped back up to the mountaintop, where Fyrian waited. He fell before his god, and opened his water-beaded hands.

"My child," Fyrian exclaimed, "what have you done? Your arms, your legs and your very life could have been shattered."

"I think it is a fair bargain," the korvi said. "Because this is from the sky. This water was flying just like I wish to."

Fyrian looked upon his child and saw a blaze. A blaze rash enough to cause harm, but capable of greatness if given the means.

"Very well," Fyrian agreed.

He gave the korvi a gift of wings, tied with powerful muscles into his back. Feathers burst outward in the colours of that korvi's inner fire. Fyrian saw also that the wings were precise things, as easily broken as a maple seed's sail. In his vast wisdom, Fyrian also gave the korvi horns, and grew them long and pointed so his children might protect their backs from flesh-hungry beasts.

"My child," Fyrian said. "You have all the gifts that are mine to give. Care now for your hurt body. You can grasp greatness in some day to come."

The korvi knew pain in his heart, then, but he agreed.

He rested for an eightday on the mountain's warm stone, and he healed as dragons do. Once his god-granted limbs were mended, he threw his new wings back and forth and discovered how to fly. For the rest of his days, that korvi flew over mountain and forest and plain, giving wings and horns to every korvi fellow he met.

Korvi were strong now, whether they walked, or climbed, or soared the skies. They spread over the land and began searching out new hearts' desires, and thus their journeys continue.

Raise

A story of Aligare

Constezza sat between him and the hearth fire, and she was a silhouette bent with the weight of care. Her shadow draped over the rock walls, the shapes of korvi horns and wings smeared like warm tar. She hummed a few notes of a festival song that Tenver could have hummed along with, in harmony.

This evening, Constezza said she would look after the egg-tending routine. Tenver didn't mind that — but now he had nothing to occupy himself but the worry that sat rife in his thoughts lately, as present as a burnt smell. He wanted more vigour in this home, more life and movement. But he couldn't figure out where to get such a thing from. Or whether a ferrin could give vigour to someone already born with fire inside them.

Tenver held his peace, sitting there curled in on himself with his tail fur for a pillow, watching Constezza work. She was partly hidden by her folded left wing, its even rows of flight quills tucked to rest against her back. Her right wingarm covered nothing: it was skinny, wrapped with a red-stitched wingsleeve that hid the scars. Without that wing's worth of feathers in the way, Tenver had only to watch Constezza's long, clawed hands splaying around eggs' surfaces. The bobbing of her loose mane feathers against her neck and horns. The minute shifting of her mouth — pulling or pressing along her dragon snout — that spoke her thoughts of how these shellbound children were faring. Minding eggs was Constezza of Veliere's calling. It was the glad-beating heart of her life but as Tenver watched the shifting of her limbs, he knew it was sedate, subtle work.

Maybe he was worrying too much, Tenver bit out within himself. Korvi folk were the toughest of the peoplekinds, gifted with long life and vital spirits. A fire could burn low and still burn. If it couldn't, there would never be breads browned over coals.

"Stubborn thing," Constezza said, trying her clawtips against the rust-coloured egg, the Iliyan family's new treasure. "Still not quickening."

"Whoever's in there needs to come out sooner or later," Tenver offered.

"Hmm," Constezza said. "That's a fistful of truth." She rose on her bird-angled legs, shuffled toward the other egg, and knelt again. If Tenver were distracted, he might have missed the particular sound of her exhalation — but he wasn't distracted and it drew his swivelling ears.

"Are you well?" Tenver asked.

"Say which, dear?" She turned her long face, one eye sliding to fix on him.

"You've been making little bits of sighs today." Standing on four feet, Tenver craned his neck concerned. "You aren't still tired, are you?"

"Ah, no," Constezza said, "not terribly."

As Tenver lolloped toward her, she tightened her bad wingarm to her back — needlessly. Tenver fit plenty well by

Constezza's right side. His whiskers arced in the space where wing feathers would be, as he sat on his haunches and looked up at her fire-shadowed face.

"My flame feels a mite low," she admitted. "Only a mite, though. Don't fret, please."

His innards dropped like falling fruit — but Tenver did as Constezza asked and believed her.

She would be fine despite the way neighbouring korvi — folk with two matching wings — had murmured in Constezza's wake some days ago, too softly for anyone but a sharp-eared ferrin to overhear. The good Veliere was walking uphill, they said, without her truest need fulfilled. They meant dragonkind's ability to fly, that tandem effort of their feathers and their fire. But Constezza had parted ways from the sky long years before Tenver was born. He could only imagine her flying, and guess at the emotions painting over her face.

"Before you suggest it," Constezza added, "I ate a whole handful of managrass seed today. Nothing's better for stoking firecasting. Wholesome stuff."

That was the sort of pleasant honey Constezza candied her dislikes with. A smile broke onto Tenver's face. "I suppose that's a start. And did you get a walk around the tunnels? A brisk one, like the healer said."

"Half of a walk, I suppose." She pursed her lips thoughtful, claws tracing the surface of the Joivenne family's egg. "I might make it up tomorrow. We need a whole medley of things."

"Oh, we'll be trading?"

"I think so. Let's hope the livelier merchants are visiting tomorrow, they can fire a person's blood just like a fine-told legend."

Tenver flexed his ears, thinking. He always felt a jump in his blood when someone stood confident on a marketplace blanket, whether it was a bard's blanket or a seller's — and Tenver didn't even have firecasting to be kindled.

"Ah," Constezza wondered, "but this was going to be your turn to try."

"No, that's fine. If you want the excitement, you should do the bartering!"

"Nonsense, you've waited like a patient stone. I'd like you to try the bartering, dear. I'd be proud as the gods themselves."

She always was that proud of him. Tenver sat there on his haunches, flexing his ears while he thought. If Constezza wanted him to try, and if a bartering session could be exciting, he might just carry two burdens in one basket. He could put fuel on Constezza's fire instead of simply sitting, fretting.

"All right. But leap into the thick of it if I start making a bad trade."

"On my eggshells," Constezza promised, wearing a mother's smile.

She finished turning the eggs, and she checked the hearth temperature again with an outspread hand. She frowned at one cooling edge; Tenver fetched shiny black coal to revive it with. Then, when all burned evenly, Constezza began the night's stories. With the eggs mutely listening, she told legends in both commontongue and korvitongue, her mouth motions like the lithe flickering of the hearth fire before her. Tenver curled up like an egg himself, his ears held high to catch every word.

Most of the legends she told were reliable favourites. The Greatbloom unfurling to create the land; the gods choosing their child races; how korvi people earned their arms and legs and wings through shows of ambition. Tenver spoke the very same words in his heart. He only recalled when he shifted position —

shifting his stubby, furred limbs and his brush-tipped tail — that he was a ferrin, a weaselkind person. Born charged with electricasting, not fire. But all things good look askance at him if he couldn't help Constezza with her flame.

In the lulls where Constezza chose which tale to tell next, Tenver wanted to suggest his own life's tale. It was no staple legend, no well-loved favourite told by bards in every village street. But the tale of Tenver Lightling, call him Tenver, had a jewel of truth inside it. Maybe it would do unhatched korvi well to hear about this ferrin fellow — so they could learn about the land's kindness.

The tale would be a simple one. Four years ago, in a Volcano tunnel town the very same as this one, there lived a korvi woman named Constezza of Veliere. She was the head of Longwick Clan and, at that particular time, she was the only member of it. Her right wing got hurt in years past and she always kept it hidden under a knit sleeve, but her remaining orange feathers and her soft-wrought smile were more than pretty enough to make it up. Constezza helped people in the Volcano to hatch their eggs, or raise their children, or nurse their sick — but mostly hatch their eggs. She was wanted and welcome everywhere she put her feet.

One day, Constezza left the Volcano, walking. The wind was mild and the Great Gem's light fell plentiful, no clouds impeding it. Carrying a sickle in her hand, Constezza walked to the plains and began cutting some tall, lush polegrass to nest other korvi's eggs with.

But soon, she heard a noise. Rustle, rustle. Something was coming closer. Constezza gathered fire in her throat and hoped it wasn't a basilisk come to snarl at her.

It wasn't: it was a ferrin. A scrawny fellow with eyes that stood out like glass shards through the polegrass. He clutched a bundle of green maple leaves to his chest and he looked up at Constezza, ears low, whiskers trembling. He asked *friend?*

Kneeling, Constezza said *yes, dear. We might be friends.* She put out an open hand for him to sniff, because that was what otherkind people did to be polite.

But the wild ferrin didn't sniff her hand. *Ten,* he said. *Ten.* He put the bundle of leaves in Constezza's offered hand, and he paused with all the land's water shining in his eyes. And then he ran back the way he came.

Constezza called after him, after the fleeing movement knifing the distant grass. The prairie wind answered her with murmuring — and the leaf bundle answered her with the tiniest of mewls. Constezza opened the bent leaves and there she found the smallest ferrin kitten she had ever seen. Curled up tight as a fern shoot, and cracking open eyes the same agate green as the ferrin who had brought him.

Standing there in the grass with a kitten in her palm, Constezza wondered what that skinny ferrin had meant when he said *ten, ten*. A gnawing thought told her that he was a wild fellow, living on what he and his mate could scratch up from the forest and the earth. That was a life some folk chose. And maybe they were blessed with ten children this litter — blessed like a plant battered to death by plentiful rain.

Constezza was far warmer than rain, with her dragon heart full of firecasting and vigor. And she had a child who needed her now, if a child with different blood. She declared to the lonely wind that she thought *ten* was a name, but not nearly enough of one. She named the kitten Tenver Lightling, so he could have that town ferrin's custom of choosing which half of his name he liked — in a future he would live to see. And as Constezza dropped maple leaves to the wind and held the shivering kitten to her fiery chest, her life became a new story altogether.

It wasn't a perfect legend, Tenver mused. It didn't have a moral as clear as chiselled stone. And it only happened four years ago: any truly great story took longer than four years to steep. And the meaning of Tenver's name was no mystery if Tenver himself knew what *ten, ten* really meant — but he felt sure that a little dishonesty helped this tale's telling.

When Constezza had told Tenver his own legend, though, she made that day sound like a story for the ages. Like nothing so plainly gloried had ever happened before in all her experience. She had lived one hundred and thirty years, which was a lot of sand-swept time but it wasn't terribly old for a korvi person. Longwick Clan's neighbours, Cherez House down the street, just lost their head fellow and he was one hundred and ninety-two. Whereas Constezza was whole lifetimes younger — ferrin lifetimes, granted — and she didn't have an illness demon plaguing her. She could still find more legends out there in the land, and she could still build her firestrength back. She had exactly one grey feather on her back, just above the base of her tail, and Tenver hadn't told her it was there yet.

So he had to try his best at bartering tomorrow morning, Tenver concluded. It was a sensation that made his heart thump and his electricasting crackle inside him, imagining himself standing tall on his haunches in the market street, playing a game of wits. But he had a working mind and a steady nerve. He knew how barter worked. Whatever Tenver ended up trading for, he was going to get some fuel for Constezza's inner fire — he was sure of it.

Morning came, a clear yellow shade of light through the ventilation hole. While Constezza preened her feathers and tended the hearth, Tenver delved into storage baskets. He selected some red cotton scraps; a big roll of leather tied sure with twine; some dried mustard leaf; clear quartz stones that somebody could stockpile their casting inside. Each item Tenver laid down on the carpet, making an ever-increasing pile.

Small barter offerings made for a challenging trade, said all the barter talk Tenver had ever listened to. If he played his wits well, he might forge the most astounding deal anyone ever spoke of. Maybe he could add firewood to his offerings. Cherez House's youngest daughter, Judellie, kept them well-stocked with wood and surely she didn't do that for every home in the Volcano. Depending on the merchant's mood and the winds of chance, hardwood sticks might be valuable trade goods, indeed.

Tenver was being terribly ambitious for someone who hadn't traded before. Doubt began chewing at his insides, but then a spoon against an iron pot lifted his ear — the harkening of Constezza making breakfast porridge. He didn't wonder again until the two of them set out for Cantrade Street.

The tunnel ceilings in Hotrock were never lower than two korvi people's heights, not with the town's many korvi people and their love of sky. But the ceiling soared even higher as they approached the market street, beyond where the light gems could illuminate far corners, and the walls fanned outward to contain all the people and sounds and smells.

"Any advice?" Tenver asked Constezza. He hurried alongside her, four-footed, the loaded pouch bouncing against his back.

Gliding on two tall legs, Constezza hummed with thought. She had smoothed her mane feathers with beeswax, and she was wearing the goldenrod yellow wrap and matching wing sleeve that made her amber feathers look an even richer hue. Festival garb, Tenver liked to think. He wondered if he should have worn his other sarong.

"No advice from me, really," Constezza said like a breeze. "I've never used hard knuckles when I barter."

"Never?"

"Well, once." She waved a hand like shooing away the possibility. "When I had a mate. We ended up with a fair trade, but I still didn't care for the process much."

"Oh. Well, it depends on who you're trading with, doesn't it?"

"It surely does. Ah, speaking of faces both new and known — there's the fellow you'll want."

Tenver followed her line of sight — to a scarlet-feathered fellow among throngs of browsing folk. He was a korvi merchant standing proud at the center of attention, his excited voice spiking above the crowd noise. His horns were short and straight, not even begun their first square-angled bend: this fellow was much younger than Constezza. He took a sack full of something from an aemet man — red hands accepting from green hands, some bargain reaching completion.

"Oh," Tenver said, "is that ...?"

"Remember Syril of Reyardine!" the merchant crowed. He fanned his wings as wide as the passing neighbour folk allowed. "Ask for the name, whatever you need!"

Tenver didn't doubt that. Around Syril's pants waistband hung three cargo pouches, all bulging with goods.

"Yes," Constezza said, "he's the new upstart everyone's talking about. Most gifted trader the Reyardines have hatched in generations, and he lends his wings to Hotrock's leader plenty often, too. They make a good pair."

As they approached, Tenver caught Syril's scent: flax oil and dusty-clean feathers, and interwoven dozens of smells from his jostling cargo pouches.

"You're ready, dear?" Constezza said it with an edge of spiced eagerness in her voice.

Yes, Tenver knew. He was ready.

Turning away from the departing aemet friend, Syril was already beaming so that his meat teeth showed — but he put on a fresher grin as he laid eyes on Constezza. "Great Ones, if it isn't a Veliere daughter!" He bowed with his wing quills and bangle-laden arms spread, the widest korvi greeting Tenver had ever seen. "Constezza, if you were an acorn in the woods, you'd be well-buried by the canniest of squirrels, my friend! It's been too many years!"

Constezza smiled, her dark eyes crinkling. "Fine to see you, too, Syril."

"How's that wing of yours?" He eyed the wingsleeve, concerned as people always were.

"Not worth speaking of. I believe this is the first time you've met my son!"

Tenver straightened as she said it, full of Constezza's own warmth. "Tenver Lightling, call me Tenver."

"Yes, yes, of course!" Syril knelt, dropping down brief to offer his hand. "Skies above, I heard birds on the wind say that Constezza of Longwick Clan had a ferrin child but I didn't dare place any wagers on—" Syril's gaze lit keenly as Tenver untied his sack of trade goods. "What have you got there, friend?"

"Plenty of things." Tenver beamed to match him. "What have you got, sir?"

Constezza was right to recommend this Reyardine fellow: he had a variety of goods most folk needed an entire home to keep, stacked expertly into his cargo pouches. Salt and thyme and firebuds came out, bound for Longwick Clan's dinner. A pigeon-blood ruby caught Tenver's eye, too, potently red in Syril's clawed grasp with its facets flashing like lightning. It reminded Tenver of the firecasting stones in the tunnelstreets' walls. Stones that could hold a person's fire, if they cared to stockpile it. Maybe Constezza could fill that ruby with her firecasting for the practice of it — or Tenver could take up firecasting, to have a heart full of fire himself. He wasn't sure which of those thoughts he liked better.

He offered Syril the mustard leaf, and quartz, and mismatched handfuls of bone and ceramic beads. Syril informed him at great length of what those goods were worth — and they were not nearly as dear as the ruby. That only made Tenver's heart dig its nails in fierce. The goods had their merits, and Tenver brought attention to them.

Constezza watched, and her barely-voiced chuckling hooked Tenver's ears, firing him onward. Soon, other folk lingered nearby, too: ferrin and korvi neighbours, and an aemet person pausing as the shape of this gathering caught her sensitive antennae. This might just be the exciting show Tenver had hoped for.

It was like a game of foursticks. Or a complicated race, toward a finish line not drawn yet. It was some sort of a show, anypace. The roll of leather was a particular prize, said Tenver's intuition, and so he held it until the end — until his and Syril's clustered piles of offerings had changed, and swelled, and changed some more.

"The point of my pitchfork," Syril announced, "is that you've nearly got a deal for me, good Tenver. But I haven't got any use for cotton bits that size and if I had to flap about to trade them, you'd need to include a heaped-full bowl of a meal to make it worth my fire."

"You've got no use for cotton, hmm?"

"I regret to say no!" Syril's grin had stopped vanishing between comments; he wore his delight plainly now.

"Then I think I can give you this, instead," Tenver said. He lifted the leather roll from within his pouch, balancing the tightly-tied heft on his arms. "More durable than any cotton grown! This leather is made from ..."

Gods only knew what kind of leather this was. Not fishleather: that was all Tenver could guess.

"... It's from the softest-skinned food creature ever to walk this land! Feel this quality, friend."

The spectators laughed in chorus as Tenver hopped nearer to Syril. Constezza's chuckle hummed among them; Tenver cocked his ears, beginning to believe he had a knack for this.

"Ah, you do speak a tall draught of truth," Syril obliged him, running his long fingers over the leather. He took the roll from Tenver, and tested its heft, and lifted the loose corner to examine the rougher side. "What a fine weight to it! Hmm."

As Syril jogged the roll in his hands, Tenver felt the crawl of forgotten information within him. He held his ears high to defy the feeling, to stifle the nervous tingle of his inner electricasting. If Syril insisted to know what kind of leather this was, Tenver had no truthful answer for him.

"That's for you, Syril," he said. "And the mustard, quartz and red clay, too. For your salt, firebuds, oilnuts and the ruby."

"Friend," Syril said, bowing low and fanning his wings grand, "I'll call the whole thing a bargain."

Relief weighed on Tenver now, as voices hummed a pleased chorus all around. The crowd dispersed, and suddenly korvi neighbours stooped toward him — to press a few copper beads and a forest plum into his hands. Payment for the entertainment, Tenver realized. Gratitude for a show cobbled together on the spot.

"Ah, kind thanks, but I'm not a bard, truly I'm not," Syril crowed while he accepted token things, too.

And then Constezza's hand fell on Tenver's back like a warmest blanket, her voice blessedly near. "What a talent you've got, my light! I haven't seen a contest like that in eightyears. Why haven't you been doing all of our barter?"

His ears wilted now, and his bravado drained away. Tenver pushed his head into her palm. "I wouldn't mind it, I don't think."

But as they walked the tunnels home, the sensation of forgotten detail still gnawed within Tenver. He turned the glassy-shining ruby in his hands, and he hoped it was nothing.

Constezza made room in the hearth embers for a stewpot and a bread pan. Dinner that day was speckled with chopped firebuds, red motes like beestings of flavour.

After minding the eggs, Constezza turned to the disarray of storage baskets and began sorting Longwick's new goods. She still fell weighty into a kneeling, perching pose but she was lasting well today; her breathing sounded nearly unremarkable and her eyes danced like embers.

"Goodness, what an exciting way to get a new stone. I'll put the ruby in with our sewing things, I suppose. Casting is a craft, too, really."

"All right. Or would it make better sense to put it in the bin of assorted precious things?"

Constezza shrugged, a lopsided motion where her scarred wing struggled to move. "Ah, it's all the same pace. Let's call it a precious thing, since it is."

Their shared quiet filled with the patting, shifting noises Constezza's hands made among everything. Then her movements came quicker and firmer. Tenver turned from scrubbing the dinner dishes with sand, feeling a significance in the air like gathering rain.

"Where did you put my shells, dear?"

The crawling sensation was back; his electricasting rose. "Your ... eggshells?"

"Mmm. They're in the blue-checked blanket, yes?"

Constezza pulled that very blanket out of a basket. It unfurled like a flag too large to fly — and it had no korvi eggshells inside. Constezza's face fell. And Tenver's guilt took shape to bite him deep: he knew the very shards of eggshell gone missing, parchment yellow on the inner curves and honey brown on the outer. They were dyed by time and probably didn't match Constezza's family colouring anymore.

"Were they," Constezza murmured, "still inside the leather roll ...?"

"Oh, gods!" Tenver darted to a basket to search, stretching over its top edge even though he knew he wouldn't find the eggshells. "I didn't even think! They were wrapped up in the blanket last time I saw them. You moved them back into the leather roll?"

"I should have told you."

"No! No, I— I should have checked." He rubbed his face wrongways. "Oh, strike me, I knew the leather felt odd, the way it was wrapped up! A-And I thought I was forgetting something, I should have just told that truth to Syril—"

Constezza's hand glided on his fur, down his neck and his hackled shoulders.

"Tenver, dear. It's just a thing."

"It's *your* thing."

She hesitated, choked with politeness. "I only need them back before I pass. There's plenty of time for that, fret not."

She needed her eggshells when her cremation day came, when her friends gathered her physical self all together and sent her heart and essence back to the fire god, Fyrian. Constezza had to return to her god: she deserved to. Those eggshells were the one earthly thing Constezza really needed and Tenver had traded them away blind.

"Frankly," she said, "I don't think the Great One would turn me away without my shells. I've never heard what he does if a korvi comes to him without." Her mouth twisted thoughtful; her hand passed again down Tenver's fur. "He'd give mercy, I'm sure."

"I didn't want to be any trouble," Tenver blurted, "I just wanted to put on a show to stir your fire!" This overdue honesty burned like a scrubbed-clean wound. "But I'll fix it! I'll— I'll go find Syril! Right now!"

And Tenver broke from Constezza's touch and ran from their home, under the door curtain and out into the tunnelstreet.

He hurried through globes of red and white light, the waning magic of the light stones in the walls. Ventilation holes let in shafts of muddy purple, night's darkcasting taking its place in the sky. Few folk walked in the market street now, only a few pairs of angled korvi legs and straight aemet legs for Tenver to dart around.

None of the korvi were Syril of Reyardine. Other merchant korvi stood tall, folding their sales blankets against their barrel chests; a lone ferrin was a quicksilver flash down the street, lolloping away. Tenver stood on his haunches for all the height he could manage, ears fanned wide — but he couldn't see the showy Reyardine, nor hear him, nor catch any trace of his scent in this smelting pot of a place.

"Looking for something, friend?" A merchant eyed him — that aemet farmer who grew herbs and seeds, and the onion greens Constezza liked. The air near him was pungent with bruised herbs, and his wares were stacked in rolled cotton for a night's storage: the aemet's spiny-knuckled hands rolled up a last bundle of sage even as he watched Tenver with wide green eyes.

"Ah, I need to find someone. It's important." With a boulder's weight of guilt, Tenver hoped not to explain. "Have you seen Syril of Reyardine? He's a red-feathered fellow, and he talks like a waterfall flows?"

"That's a fine way to describe everyone in Reyardine House," the merchant chuckled. "Syril, though? He hasn't been here for hours. He was saying something about getting to East Hotrock before nightfall."

"Oh," Tenver breathed. Craning back, he looked out the ventilation shaft overhead — knowing he wouldn't see the flying person he needed but hoping keenly anyway. "Burn my luck ..."

"That good Reyardine is the most vigorous trader of his whole family line," the merchant said, his voice leaden with regret. He shook his head, antennae swaying over his head like two sapling branches. "You'll need to borrow someone's wings, unless you've got feet as quick as the wind."

No ferrin in the land had feet that quick, enough to catch up to a korvi in soaring flight. Tenver could nearly feel Constezza's eggshells far in the distance, vanished into the surrounding land and all its multitude, and it was a crushing thing to imagine.

"But if it helps you any," the merchant added, "I've heard tell that Syril of Reyardine runs errands for Tijo." He said Tijo's name as aemet tongues always said korvi names: as firm sounds, unblended. "If you don't manage to find the good Reyardine on your own, you might ask our head mage."

Their head mage who didn't live in South Hotrock, but in an entirely different section of tunneltown. More distance. The eggshells slipped farther away with each heartbeat. Tenver nodded, ears sinking toward his neck, and he thanked the merchant.

"Gods help you, friend," came the kind-frowning reply. And the merchant turned back to his rolling and tying work.

Tenver hoped not to see any more bundles tonight. He lolloped back toward home, numb — but yet thinking.

The tunnelstreets emptied around Tenver. Only a few neighbours caught sight of him, and they offered uneasy, hopeful smiles instead of voiced greetings. Wood scent grew stronger as Tenver neared home — the dry hardwood smell that meant Judellie of Cherez had stopped by with an armload of firewood. The ordinariness chafed against Tenver's gathering thoughts.

Constezza had retired to bed already. She was a calm mound ready for sleep, her tail and legs buried under a blanket, her sleek wing and her scar-patterned wingarm both catching the hearth coals' light. She raised her chin from the bed mat. "Any good fortune?"

His ears rested on his neck already; they couldn't fall any lower. "No," he said.

"Dear, really, it's fine."

"I'll go travelling and find Syril."

"It's not that broad a trouble ... We can ask folk to pass a message to the good Syril of Reyardine next time they catch sight of him. Someone is bound to speak with him again soon. There's no call for you to go running about."

"No, but there is," Tenver blurted. "What if he doesn't come back here for a while? Or— Or if he trades the leather to someone else?" Dread coiled around Tenver's heart, the feeling of more unknowns levering Constezza's eggshells away from her.

Shifting within her blanket refuge, folding her arms and propping her long-jawed head on top, Constezza sighed. She looked tired, suddenly. A weariness she usually buried under kind busywork, but now it was revealed, more real and life-worn than Tenver had ever thought.

"Imagine if Syril goes flapping around in the eastern land for a while," Constezza said, speculating as light as air. Her gaze slid to Tenver, mild under lowered lids. "If a bad luck demon has snatched my shells up, it could take a year. Maybe two."

"I hope that's a rake without teeth," Tenver hurried to say.

Constezza laughed. "What's a few years for dragonkind? Did I ever tell you that my grandfather lived two hundred and fifty-five whole years?"

Tenver's eyes bugged. "That's— That's really old for your kind, isn't it?"

"Oh, yes. He couldn't fly for the last few eightyears, but that was it! Still sturdy as a steel hammer. We told him we'd start spinning legends about the korvi who lived forever — so I think he must have died of spite."

Such spans of time. All of it was far distant, a painted scene others told Tenver about because he could never truly see it. Tenver Lightling, call him Tenver, might see twenty years all grouped together if he was fortunate: he was a korvi's son but not really.

And in this moment, he wanted nothing more than to die before Constezza, to grow old knowing she was still well and full of fire. That everything was going to be all right for her.

That she had everything she was owed. That was a truth swelling painful inside Tenver — while he held his ears level, as though his feelings were smooth, neutral things.

"So the point of my nail is that we've got time," Constezza went on. "Syril isn't one to hide in a crevice somewhere. We'll find those shells — don't you fret for a moment."

Looking to his own toes under his sarong's edge, Tenver nodded. He lolloped to Constezza's bedside and breathed in her scent. "I'm still going to fix this, though. First thing in the morning. Somebody said I go should ask Tijo — he'll know where I can find Syril of Reyardine."

With a tightening of lips all along her snout, Constezza laid her hand over Tenver's neck. "Well. If you think it's best, dear."

"I do."

"We can call it your own journey. My child leaving to see the land ..."

He nudged her wrist; the contact was a balm to his inner strife. It lasted a long moment before Constezza took her hand back, and before Tenver headed for the nest of bunched-up cloth that was his own bed.

Constezza wormed back to comfort, the bedclothes rustling. "Speaking of folk flapping off on journeys, Judellie stopped by while you were gone. Said she was travelling — and the young thing looked nervous, so I didn't pry at her. She brought enough firewood for a three-day Lifedancing, though, so I'll have plenty of fuel while you're out."

"Hmm," Tenver replied. Curled and unmoving, his tail brush pillowing his head, he now noticed the looming shadow of the woodpile. "There must be a travelling wind, if we're both leaving."

"Seems so! It's about time she travelled. Thirty-some years old and she's been here for every day of it, regular as dawn and dusk. Maybe she should have the healer check her fire, too."

Tenver folded his ears. Not that Constezza noticed: her profile was peaceful, eyes closed, a smile sliding along her face.

"And before you speak one word about it, Tenver, yes — I'll pay close mind to my fire while you're away. One hour each day spent walking, banish me if I don't. And I'll see about some more managrass. Brewed into a tonic, maybe ... That way, I can put honey in it."

She knew Tenver like the roof of her own mouth. He smiled into his tail fur. "And wholesome vegetables with your dinner, too. Green ones. Can you promise me?"

"On my eggshells."

She wouldn't break a promise, wherever her shells were. Tenver listened as Constezza fidgeted to rest, as her breathing evened.

But he laid there in the quiet, listening to the tranquil crackling of the hearth coals, and he didn't sleep. Thinking of those eggshells' faded colours did sting his heart.

In midnight's thickest purple, Tenver left his home. He carried some chestnuts to eat and another handful of trade trinkets just in case, tied together in a fire-coloured blanket on his back. If he couldn't sleep, then he could chase his mistake away into the dark.

Hotrock's tunnels spread away vacant, a far different collection of places than during the day. People's scents held weak in the air, mingling with the dust like powdered paints spread too thin. Tenver's pattering footfalls reached the vaulted ceilings. He saw his own shadow sometimes when he passed fading light gems, and that was nearly like company.

The walls and corners grew less familiar after half an hour's journeying. Tenver had never been to the eastern settlement of the Volcano — only to the farthest reaches of South Hotrock's corridors, and outside into its sparse maple forests. In these new corridors, Tenver followed the patterned flags that decorated the ceilings of travelling streets. He eyed ventilation holes and guessed how near he was to the mountainous outer surface. Plenty of folk travelled between the four sides of the Volcano, Tenver soothed himself. Even folk who couldn't fly. It couldn't be a challenge too tightly knotted for him to handle.

And he was making quick time in these empty tunnels, without pausing to check for oncoming folk, without sideways hops to evade handcarts and people carrying unwieldy pigeon cages. As Tenver's limbs tired and his paws grew numb from the running, he imagined a measure of circumference behind him, a good fraction of the Volcano's great, round span passed by.

He paused in a street with flags shaped like bird silhouettes, flat crows and chakdaws flying motionless on the tunnel ceiling. The space was wide enough for three korvi to spread their wings fully and not touch feathers — a social street, likely. This was someplace people collected like pooling rainwater to share whatever gossip East Hotrock saw in a day. Tenver hopped to a communal water bucket tucked away in the corner, and drank from its ladle, finding the water was stale but welcome.

Overhead was a skylight opening for korvi folk to land through, like an enormously wide ventilation hole. Tenver sat there on his haunches and watched the rich purple smear of the sky. Pale patches glided past, the distant clouds that ferrinkind eyes weren't very good at discerning.

The sky was something Tenver couldn't reach, not on his own. Not even if he learned firecasting and held it in his heart.

He would need wings first. Maybe someday, if a samekind person was ambitious enough, ferrin could get their own wings from goddess Ambri, but that wasn't going to help Tenver today. What an odd idea, Tenver thought, savouring the truth of it like a bitter candy. He wasn't even sure he liked the thought of travelling through the entire sky full of wind.

He ate one of his stored chestnuts. And he sat there for a while, beside a water pail built by a stranger. Fatigue soaked him now — but he could find the East Hotrock mage home before he stopped to rest, he was waveringly sure. He adjusted the blanket's tension around his chest and retied his slipping sarong, and he kept on.

The tunnel bends came quicker now that he was within the real town part of East Hotrock. More tunnelstreets branched away, and more curtain-covered doorways passed by. And there were black ink splotches on the walls, to help a person navigate. Tenver wasn't familiar with any of these markings — just the colourful paint blotches back home — and he pushed on down the most worn-looking paths, along the most muddled trails of people's scents. Those would surely lead to the heart of the town. At the heart of any town were the wisest, kindest, most skilled people and if they weren't named the mages or leaders, they would at least know who was.

There was no one around to ask at this hour. Darklight still fell through the ventilation holes and through the great skylights passing overhead, a dingy shade of violet. Clear yellow dawn was hours away. With a twisting in his innards, Tenver was beginning to regret his haste. He stood breathing hard in a strange-scented place, among untold numbers of sleeping folk — and waking someone up wouldn't get Constezza's shells back. No korvi flew in the dark depth of night.

It was another mistake, said the hollow sadness in Tenver's chest. He should have had a mote of patience. Should have thought his plan over and brooded on it. He untied the blanket and arranged its contents to one side, so some of the soft expanse was free for Tenver to lie on. He curled around himself and looked at the far-off ceiling, as though he could carve it into his memory, like korvi miners had carved these very walls. All he could do was wait and regret.

Tenver woke to voices, murmuring like river water around him. Someone stood near him — not smelling like home, not like Constezza. It was a ferrin person only familiar to Tenver's samekind bones.

"Friend?" she said again. "Wake up, please."

"Hmm?" Tenver rose and scrubbed at his face fur. Movement whisked by — korvi walking past, turning mild glances toward him.

"That's a curious place to sleep," the other ferrin said. She was black-furred and white-tipped, with her ears quirked as uneven as her smile. "You've caused some kind of a stir! Folk have been asking each other if they know you. Four dozen neighbours must have come by to look at you and see if they knew your face."

Tenver grinned an apology, as he gathered his makeshift bed back into a tied bundle. "At least they'll have something fresh to talk about, I suppose. I was travelling late. Great Dark took good care of me."

A flash caught his eye — from a gemstone in the other ferrin's collar, a yellow stone snatching light as she tilted her head.

"Oh," Tenver blurted, "that's— You're a mageling, aren't you?"

"I am!" She beamed like daybright. "And you're here for something important, I'm sure. Is it healing casting?"

"Ah, no. I need to find someone. A son of Reyardine House."

Her ears fell into studious folds. "I can't help you, then. You'll want Tijo. You're sure you don't need healing casting? I have bright and dark."

"No, thank you."

"You'll want Tijo," the mageling amended, "or maybe else someone he knows. This way, please!"

The mageling lolloped brisk through the tunnels, weaving between the taller peoplekinds, and Tenver followed her bouncing tailtip. People gathered in clusters as they neared Tijo; many of them were sharing gossip in hushed voices. A few passed around green herbs or tincture bottles with leaves drawn on them. Remedies recommended by the mage, maybe.

They ducked under a door curtain, one embroidered heavy with colours. Here was a circular chamber — not a home like Tenver expected. It was too large, and it couldn't be a home without a hearth fire. Light stones lined the chamber walls, their crystal facets releasing darkcasting light like brambleberry syrup suspended in the air.

Up ahead stood a korvi man with his winged back to Tenver, speaking to someone before him. He held his wine-coloured wings folded tight; his length of tail touched the floor but didn't support weight. He looked sure and yet relaxed. Which seemed like a good demeanor for a mage serving the thousands of people in Hotrock Volcano, sorting out their troubles like picking seeds from chaff.

Tijo was speaking in a voice as calm as water. Korvitongue words reached Tenver's ears — too distant to make out at first, but then the sounds sharpened into rolling words.

"Vre parivrepa liz vrunun-ea karvri sa nul—"

I wager that we-can maybe change that thing, Tenver worked out in halting mindvoice. He fanned his ears wide to catch every nuance of tongue; he rarely spoke korvi words himself, but he listened to Constezza's korvitongue legends plenty often. Comprehension would catch up to him soon enough.

Once they stopped at Tijo's feet, the mageling sat tall on her haunches.

"Tijo? I found another traveller seeking you."

Snapping his mouth mildly shut, Tijo of Fideless turned to face them.

"Good morning," he said. He clutched a mug of drink that seemed forgotten even while he held it, while he ran considering eyes over Tenver. "A busy morning, at that ... Thank you."

The mageling showed satisfaction in her eyes and in the cant of her ears. With a glance to Tenver, she left.

"I'll see to you in a moment," Tijo said, "if that's well."

"*Fine for me,*" Tenver replied in korvitongue.

Hurrying a smile — his relief at Tenver not minding the otherkind language — Tijo turned back to his first visitor.

"Commontongue is good for me," the visitor said — with a thick dressing of korvitongue accent, a crisp female voice that Tenver recognized. "And I think he prefers commontongue, maybe."

"Is that—" Tenver asked. "Judellie?"

She leaned past Tijo's wing, bright red and young-faced, fanning her wings a featherwidth in greeting: she was a delightful sight so far from home. "Fine to see you, Tenver!"

Her smile bent oddly, though. Crimped with a worry Tenver barely noticed, but his ferrinkind gut latched onto.

Tijo raised brows. "Ah, you folk know each other?"

"We're neighbours," Tenver said. He hopped closer and returned to straight-backed attentiveness. "Nearly next-door neighbours. I think we passed within a hair's width of each other, if we both left last night ... "

"Hmm." Tijo ran an appraising eye over both of them, millwheels turning behind his eyes. "You're both stoked hot enough to forego sleep? I'd imagine you'll make a good pair. Tenver, is it?"

"That's right. Tenver Lightling, call me Tenver, of Longwick Clan."

"Ah, Longwick. I've heard about the good Constezza. What is it you're here for?"

While shaking Tijo's offered hand between his own little pale ones, while noticing his canvas-stout scent, Tenver's ears dropped before he could stop them. He looked at the floor since he couldn't hold Tijo's even gaze. "I'm. I'm here to borrow someone else's wings. I made a mistake and— I traded something away that I shouldn't have traded, so I have to go get it back."

"Traded? To whom?"

"A merchant fellow, he was visiting South Hotrock yesterday. Do you know Syril of Reyardine?"

Tijo let out a weary breath — but he smiled, too, letting a white sliver of tooth show. "You're trying to catch up to Syril of Reyardine, owner of the quickest wings this side of the land?"

"He's really that fast?!"

"I'm surprised he didn't tell you that," Tijo said, dry.

"Oh, no ... I really need to see him before he trades away the goods he's carrying."

Judellie inflated in the corner of his vision, her chest swelling full of a deep breath as she thought. "If it helps you, Tijo," she ventured, "I can fly two errands together. Bring

Tenver where he is going, maybe, and deliver something for you ...?"

She looked both more nervous than Tenver had ever seen her, but more determined, too. Set firmer in her own heart's cement.

Tijo turned the leaderly expression on her, that look of measuring of quantities — while another collar-wearing ferrin approached four-footed, bouncing to a halt at Tijo's feet.

"Tijo? We're ready for the lesson."

"It's that time already?" Frowning, choosing one path over another, Tijo turned a last time to Tenver and Judellie. "Very well. I'll make a team of you two. Judellie, take Tenver and head for Plainsreach town, if you would. Last I spoke with Syril of Reyardine, he was headed to Plainsreach today at first bright — but he commonly leaves town an eightmoment before he says he's planning to. That dear fool just can't stay put." With a wisp of a smile, Tijo continued, "Go by wings. South-west, toward green fields. Fly with all your fire and keep your eyes open — you might chance upon the good Reyardine before he can flap off elsewhere."

Judellie nodded, a hurried jerk of a motion.

Canting his head, Tijo said, "Luckily for you, I've got a message that needs carrying to Plainsreach. Ready? Here's what you'll bring to the mage."

In that anticipating moment, Tenver imagined a message about a thousand interwoven affairs. But Tijo only asked them to propose a simple trade: Plainsreach's spinach harvest for any ores Hotrock might offer. Iron, particularly.

Without any further delay, Tijo bade his ferrin mageling to get a carrying pouch. That collared fellow left and returned with a thick cotton sack, one with a strap and three compartments Tenver could fit inside.

Judellie looped the strap over her head, arranging it between her armshoulders and wingshoulders. And then she held the pouch open, offering.

Tenver was going to be carried by a korvi — one who could fly. He felt the truth of this bargain at his throat now, like a newly worn scarf pulled a little too tight. But he climbed into the sackcloth, and then he was a flag strung from Judellie's shoulders, bouncing against her strong chest as she leaped and flapped upward.

He spent a long moment getting used to the gut-churning motion of flight — but already they were falling, and jerking to a halt against the ground. Tenver poked his head out of the fabric to see the open sky, eye-wateringly bright, with Hotrock Volcano's surrounding plains as a patchwork of terrain colours in the blurry distance. Clouds moved sluggish; the wind over the bare face of the Volcano was mild and it made no sound.

Judellie stood looking outward. Overhead, her throat worked as she swallowed. "I need to be sure of where I'm going," she said, "before I begin flying."

"That's a reasonable thing to check." Tenver dug into his packed things, finding the shape of a chestnut and closing grasp around it. "Are you hungry?"

"Mmm? No. Thank you."

He chewed. Such a mundane action in a place like this, on the wind-scoured slope of the Volcano.

"I might take your kindness later," Judellie said. "It will be fuel for my fire." She angled her head toward Tenver, one dark eye landing on him. "That makes sense in commontongue, yes? Fuel for my fire?"

"That's right. Your commontongue is getting better!"

"Ah," Judellie protested, her body bunching into a shrug. "It is not better enough. If I forget some words ..."

Tenver had seen aemet farmers in the Volcano listening to a rolling string of korvitongue speech, and then giving a commontongue answer. They could never speak the dragon language with their betweenkind mouths, but ears weren't so choosy. Outside of the Volcano, though, Constezza said that aemets typically lived with just a few korvi folk — so they didn't learn korvitongue at all. They didn't need it in their fields and forests, close to their plant friends and their bug cousins.

Judellie hadn't left the Volcano to see the land, so she had yet to meet those other folk. Even though her flight quills were all grown in, and even though her horns grew longer every year. She had barely left the Cherez House home in the time Tenver knew her, only visiting the Volcano slope forests that yielded firewood. Judellie had mostly stayed near her croaking-voiced grandfather and applied medicinal things to the demon-made sores that gradually wrung him out: she was out in the daylight now but she hadn't looked this tight around the mouth since the day of the funeral pyre.

A pyre with eggshells on it, whispered Tenver's guilt.

"Is that what you came to Tijo for?" he asked Judellie, wanting again to hurry away from here. "To get sent somewhere?"

"Yes. Yesterday, I thought that ... I should go travelling. It has been enough time."

She wasn't telling the entire lump of truth. Which was a ferrin thing to think.

Not everyone can see the body's messages so easily, Constezza said in his mind, a trace of firelit past. *Make sure you oblige folk.*

Flexing his ears, Tenver tried lightly, "Well, today is the best day to begin something. If you want me to translate or anything else, you can just ask."

"I might need that favour," Judellie said. "Plainsreach is south-west ... Yes?"

"That's right." Tenver pulled papery skin off his remaining bite of chestnut and dropped it, letting it swirl away on the entire sky's wind.

Judellie shifted her wings, smooth rustling motions that were nothing like taking off. "You ... traded something you shouldn't have traded?"

"Yeah, I made a mess." He swallowed his unease: Judellie deserved to know why she was doing Tenver this favour. "I accidentally traded Constezza's eggshells away."

"Oh, gods! Is she ..." Judellie paused sudden. "Is she worried?"

"Not really. I mean, not that she showed ... She said it was fine, but I just don't think she—"

Tenver willed his fur smooth against him, and pulled his spreading electricasting back toward the core of his being. If he kept feeling so fear-touched, he might accidentally loose his electricity on Judellie.

"I just think a day without her eggshells is too much. It's the spirit of the thing, you see? They're hers, and she needs them back. This wouldn't be a trouble we need to think about, if it weren't for my mistake."

"Ah... That is a reasonable thing to flap over. My eggshells are safe in my mother and father's ... *vigeler*?"

Tenver considered word meanings, his ears folding. "Ah ... Guardianship?"

"Guardianship! Thank you. My shells are in my mother and father's guardianship, but I do not think that will be true for much longer. My own eggshells might not be safe with me unless I am sure and responsible. You see?"

It was Tenver's turn to hum a sympathy sound. "I've got a suggestion: don't wrap them up in a material that doesn't look important."

"No, no. I will have them made into beads, maybe." Her silence seemed like the other half of her thought. She opened and resettled her wings, shaking out her tension like so much dust. With another pause, and a glance to Tenver, she adjusted the carrying pouch around him. "We should leave. Syril flies as fast as Tijo says. I lost a race to him once."

"You did?" Tenver couldn't picture Judellie doing a blaze-hearted thing like accepting a wager.

"He is only a little older than me." She shrugged the idea away. "I will fly as fast as I can. Apologies for the wind."

There was nothing left but for Tenver to sink back inside the pouch.

He had never thought about korvi carrying their weaselkind friends before. It was simply a fact of the land, an arrangement people made sometimes. But sitting in the carrying pouch, with his fur and whiskers mashed against his body, had a tone of reality to it that Tenver didn't believe he liked. He stuck his head out once. The wind battered his whiskers and screamed in his ears and dried out his eyes: he withdrew back into the pouch. Now he understood Judellie's apology for the wind.

Constezza must have missed that flight wind. It must have stroked her hide and feathers, and fanned her fire. She probably used to enjoy the wind in those years long since slipped away. She might have played in the air like a fledgling crow, wheeling and diving for the joy of it; she had never said as much but Tenver imagined it was true.

Time seeped past, until Judellie said over the wind that they were arriving in Plainsreach. They descended, and Tenver felt both lighter and heavier until Judellie jarred against the ground.

He squirmed out of the carrying pouch, leaving his blanket satchel inside because he didn't want that constriction, either: Tenver hopped onto the dusty street and hurriedly groomed his fur to order.

"Here we are," Judellie told him. "We will find the Reyardine in the market street, maybe."

"That's where I found him in Hotrock," Tenver agreed. He tugged his sarong straight and paid proper attention to Plainsreach now: it was a wide-open place under plentiful sky, with grass thatch buildings lining both sides of the street. Horse droppings and burning cornstalks and torn mint leaves clung to the wind. Aemets passed by, turning curious eyes to Tenver but mostly to Judellie: they wondered what brought her here, since some errand or endeavour clearly had.

"I do not see him," Judellie ventured. She turned a long-piercing gaze down the street, considering the vendors at the far end of the street. But as a pair of aemets walked past, the concentration faded; Judellie glanced to them and didn't say anything, wearing her dilemma as plain as her own feathers.

"Excuse me, friends," Tenver called, hopping forward. "Do you know if Syril of Reyardine been here today?"

The aemets paused, antennae cutting the air as they turned to confer with each other.

"Ah," the man said. "I don't recall the name ..."

"He's a red-feathered fellow with young horns? A merchant ...?" Tenver stood on two legs and his tail like a korvi would, spreading his arms wide and thinking of vivid bartering courage. "He says things like: welcome, friends, and a fine bundle of the day's best to you!"

The two aemets smiled crooked with bemusement; the woman nudged her companion and wondered, "The Reyardines are all like that, aren't they? Bright blossoms in the field. Ah, but I did see somebody like that today! It seemed that he was trading with the Newwin family? Ask Sage, she might have a better scrap of information for you."

"That's fine and well! Thank you."

They nodded, and shifted to leave.

"Oh, and one more thing," Tenver added, "if I might ask! Where can we find your mage?"

Plainsreach had only one mage, an aemet woman who invited them into her house in a trilling bird's voice. Tenver supposed that if this town was small enough to fit everyone on one main street, they wouldn't need the relays of magelings and leaders who helped Tijo manage matters. This one person named the mage would be plenty.

"Your turn," Tenver told Judellie, murmured against the liquid surface of his drink. The mage had poured him a generous cupful of berry mull; it smelled delicious enough that Tenver considered drinking the entire overlarge portion.

The mage watched Judellie, expectant. So after a pause to comb her memory and set down her own cup, Judellie began.

Tenver recalled the words of the bargain, clear as a tapped tonebox. Tijo hoped that this message found the mage well; he heard that the harvests had been generous this year; and he wanted to see about trading Plainsway's spinach for Hotrock's ores, particularly iron. Tenver winced inside as he listened to Judellie stammer through that list of worded sentiments, and he tried to hold himself neutral.

"Your spinach harvest," Judellie concluded, "For ... Hotrock's iron ore goods."

The mage blinked while she filed thoughts away. "Iron or goods? What kind of goods?"

"Ah," Judellie ventured. She opened her mouth and nothing came off her long tongue.

"Hotrock's iron ore," Tenver offered. "All the goods that are ... ore."

"That is a strange mix of words," Judellie wondered.

The mage hummed agreement, staring into the air while she thought. And she gave an answer to carry back: Plainsreach didn't have a smelting korvi any longer, so their metalwork would be done by plantcasting folk. No raw ores. She wished to know what else Hotrock could offer — for twenty piled bushels of fine spinach.

"You can carry that message back?" the mage asked them both.

"Yes, we will," Judellie said, sure.

"But while we're here," Tenver added, "We need to speak with one of your townsfolk. If you wouldn't mind saying where we can find her."

As they left the home, Judellie released a sigh, one that must have been pent up in the deepest reaches of her barrel chest. "Iron or ore ... I would not have known how to explain that. I owe you a basket of plums. Or some plum wine. My nerves could use the wine."

Tenver lolloped beside her, smiling with lax ears. "You don't owe me a thing, I'm still relying on your wings! But, say — when we get back, let's ask Constezza about her reserve of brandy. It'll be a glad enough day to bring it out. If we can actually find her shells, I mean ..."

They carried on down the street, past thatch walls and door curtains stirring in the wind. An aemet swept the street dirt outside her door with a cornstalk broom, revealing a darker swath of earth; she paused to let Tenver and Judellie pass unbothered.

"Although," Tenver added, "it won't really be a celebration. It'll just be my mistake not being a mistake anymore."

"I saw you trading that day. With Syril."

He looked up at Judellie, past the pants-clad motion of her long legs. "You were in the market?" He should have noticed Judellie nearby — or not, since he was so absorbed in his bartering show, that dance of words with the good Reyardine.

"Mmm. I was just passing through the market. I did not know you bartered. And ..." She hesitated, and then spoke in a low, hurried korvitongue. *"There you lived-and-breathed, pace-keeping with Syril. That gave me a thought that I should not be hundred-fold scared. Thirty-one years inside me and I had not even left the Volcano! Why does this dragon have wings if she is really a snake?"* Muscles stood tight along her jaw; she glanced guilty toward the aemet locals, who were paying no mind to her otherkind words.

Tenver ventured, "So, you left in the night because you didn't want to wait?"

"I waited enough," she replied. And then she turned sharp, and rapped knuckles on a slanted door pole. They had reached the home of the Newwin family, the next folk to borrow help from.

An aemet woman came, lifting the door curtain with her elbow, guarding the ball of herb-speckled dough she held. She was Sage Newwin, she said, still digging her blunt knuckle spines into the dough, the herbs' peppery scent escaping with each movement.

"Yeah, Syril of Reyardine is long gone," she said. "I made a few trades with him, just for some pantry bits and odds, and then saw him flapping off this way." She pointed skyward with a dough-caked finger, drawing a line from west to east. "I couldn't say where he was going. Haven't laid ears on that news."

"Oh." The despair rushed back in; Tenver felt distance closing in on him. "Do you know anyone who ... who might know?"

"We are trying to find a thing Syril carries," Judellie tried. "It— It is a piece of leather with eggshells inside."

"Leather? A big, rolled-up piece? We bartered that from him, actually."

Tenver's heart leaped and his ears matched it.

"There might have been someone's eggshells in it," Sage went on, a thinking frown worming across her face. "Chive didn't unroll it to see. She's the one who wanted that leather — gods know why. Some project off in the field. Hope it's something she's having fun with, anypace."

"Could— Could we talk to Chive about it?"

Smiling and wincing together, Sage said, "If you can find her."

The Newwin family was well-established in Plainsreach, and known for their baking; so said the Plainsreach mage when Tenver had asked. While Tenver and Judellie visited, they might see about some bread, or biscuits, or tin-oven cakes. Most of the Newwins practiced that edible craft – except for Chive. Chive foraged. That was all the mage had to say about it and the remark thudded strangely in the air.

That simplicity nagged at Tenver, while he sat in the carrying pouch again. Judellie glided in circles, winding slowly outward over the plains. Her eyes were best for the task of searching: Tenver hoped she would find the green aemet woman amid the green grass — soon, or at all.

"Tenver?" she said, after long moments. "Look with me, will you?"

The thought unsettled his innards — but he shoved his head free anypace, and gripped the pouch's edge while he looked down. There wasn't so much wind this time, in this more vigilant style of flight, but he still squinted.

"I don't have flight eyes, though." Land blurred past in green and yellow rivulets. They were higher above the earth than any treetop Tenver had ever seen, let alone any tree he had ever climbed. "Sage said she's wearing a brown tunic and leggings. So we can watch for that, I'd wager."

"Brown. All right."

"And if she's foraging for things, she'll be ..." Tenver wondered whether grass or trees would be more telling features to a forager. Or some other aspect of the sprawling land. "Actually, I'm not sure where foragers go. Wherever food is?"

Judellie hissed a frustrated sound; smoke scent touched the air while she exhaled. "I should fly higher and look at all things, maybe."

She did just that, wings slapping the air. The land's smeared colours smeared even more. Tenver took a tighter grip on the pouch fabric, the only thing close enough to be real.

"I wonder what kind of food she forages for," Tenver thought aloud. "Herbs, maybe? Sage was using them in that bread dough. But there are plenty of gardens and fields in Plainsreach, so why forage for herbs?"

Judellie made a gruff curiosity sound. "She forages for honey, maybe? Or— Or something else for cooking?"

"Probably anything she can find." Tenver folded his ears, considering all the seasonings and food staples he had ever known. Plenty of them were leaves, stems or roots. "She might be bending down low, to pick things?"

Judellie hummed again. "So I will see her bending back, maybe. Not her head and her— Her long things."

"Antennae."

"Thank you." Judellie raised her hands against the wind, her hands crisp and near as they shaped a curve like an aemet's shelled back. "I might see a shape like this."

"Yeah. And she has the roll of leather, too! It's big, and brown, and a particular shape. I don't know what she's using it for — maybe you'll be able to sight that."

"I will try."

A hopeful quiet fell between them, broken by the rushing air each time Judellie banked. She sailed a little closer to the ground, so that threads of dark texture broke through the blur, and occasional white and blue motes that might have been flowers. Tenver was still no use in keeping watch. But he left his head out and his ears folded against the wind: retreating into the pouch seemed like turning fully away, and he was too stoked full of hope to do that.

"There!" Judellie suddenly cried. "Down there!"

She banked, spiralling hard. The ground tilted and grass tops rushed toward them, distinct and many. Tenver caught a glimpse of what Judellie must have meant: a personshape in brown clothing, low to the ground. Not stooped over — but lying down.

Judellie landed, battering the tall grass with her wingbeats and jolting to a stop. She heaved a deep breath and began crouching but Tenver was already jumping out of the pouch to land on crunching grass: something about that glimpsed aemetshape was stirring electric worry inside him.

"Hello?" Tenver called. "Chive ...?"

"That is indeed my name," came a reedy groan.

Tenver wedged his nose through the grass stems, emerging onto bald earth. Chive lay face-down, her round face resting on her bent elbow — and her other hand clutching a wet streak on her tunic-clad side.

Electricasting arced inside Tenver as he bolted closer. "Goodness, are you all right?! Judellie!"

"Thank everything you're here, new friends." Chive held a pinch of tunic fabric in her insect-spined fingers, dabbing what was underneath. "I can't see to pour water on it. Can't waste it."

"Pour water on ...?"

Judellie joined Tenver at Chive's side now, kneeling and tucking her wings tight: she saw the wet stain and she turned bowl-wide eyes to Tenver, a look that matched his feelings perfectly.

"Just. Here." Chive yanked up the edge of her tunic.

Tenver's fur bristled electric as he expected an awful scene — but there was plenty of unbroken, pond-green skin. The wound gaped between her insectkind shell plates and her furkind flesh, glistening wet and leaking threads of blue blood — thankfully only threads.

Judellie hissed sympathy. She took the tunic's edge. "What happened?"

"I fell on a salt crystal. Landed on the sharp edge. Salt's in there well and deep. Please, the water."

She lifted a water pouch, a little waxcloth shape Tenver hadn't even noticed in the crook of her curled arm. Judellie took it and eyed the wound. With a cautious hand, she poured a shimmering wire of water.

Tenver had nothing to do but watch, and squirm, and will his electricasting back toward his core. After a fidgeting moment, he hopped closer to Chive's head. She stared at air just beyond the curve of her face. Single hairs had escaped her four braids, and they wafted disordered.

"Uh, so, you're a Newwin daughter," he asked, "isn't that right?"

"That's me." She smiled wry. Between the tapering bases of her antennae, sweat sat beaded on her forehead, more than Tenver had never seen or scented on a betweenkind person. "My sister sent you?"

"Well, she told us where to look for you. Um, I'm Tenver Lightling, call me Tenver. She's Judellie. It's a big heap of luck that we found you!"

"Move, please," Judellie said. "This way."

Rolling obediently, Chive sighed, "Try to put together a surprise and this is what I get."

"You fell on salt rocks ...? Where?"

"Heh! I said it was a surprise." Wearing a soggy grin, Chive lifted an arm and pointed toward her feet.

Tenver saw nothing there but bent grass among loosened earth. Then he noticed darkness. Darkness like a cave mouth. He hopped closer on all fours and the hole grew, spreading down into the earth. Dozens of body-lengths away in the darkness, squares glittered in multitudes — like crystal facets.

"See the salt?" Chive asked. "Hidden down there, quiet as rootstalks. I came across it like that, all opened up. I think cavebirds must have been digging a nest and found that gap in the earth. Be careful, Tenver — don't fall."

He put his belly to the earth, stretching his neck to see the glittering far below. Tenver once got cooking vinegar in a cut on his hand; he didn't relish the thought of trying salt.

"But really," Chive went on, breathless yet cheerful, "despite this unpleasantness, I was so lucky to find that cave! Imagine everyone's faces when I bring back bushels and bushels of salt!"

"It'll make for wonderful trades," Tenver admitted.

The glittering salt facets reminded him of his ruby back home — and beside the hole he noticed another familiar sight. It was the roll of leather, half-opened but still the very same. Heart bursting, Tenver hopped to it. Chive hadn't unfolded it fully: the cotton inner wrapping was untouched, and inside those layers were the eggshell shards — warmly yellow and brown, smelling of home. They truly were a piece of Constezza, Tenver felt as he rewrapped the cotton, hiding the treasure once again.

"That is all I can do," Judellie reported. A twist cap clicked on the water flask. "It feels less bad?"

"Feels strange." Chive shifted against the grass. "Doesn't burn anymore, though. I owe you the land, Judellie."

"You should not move it, maybe."

"Nngh. I think you're right."

"The mage should see this — you need healing casting, I think." Judellie turned her face toward Tenver, a long movement in the corner of his vision. "Tenver? You found them?"

"I did." He finished tying the cotton wrap's corners into a reliable bundle.

"Let me see if I can—" Chive's words crumbled into a gasp, and she sagged back to earth.

"Your shell is like your backbone, isn't it?" Tenver seemed to recall that, from his vague idea of how aemets' two-kind bodies worked. "Don't move it around, Chive."

"Sounds like good sense." She pressed her lips. "I've got to get home sometime, though."

Surrounded by the endless murmur of plains grass, the three of them met each other's wide eyes.

"I would not mind carrying you," Judellie began.

They three discussed it, sitting there in the open daybright. The cautious decision was that if Chive shouldn't walk, then she shouldn't move at all. But the leather she bartered for could still be a carrying aid; Chive rolled carefully into the middle and Judellie picked up the edges. The leather held taut while Judellie tried the balance of it, wiggling her fisted grip back and forth.

"Strong arms you have!" Chive twisted her shell-backed neck, trying to lay eyes on the entire sling that held her. "Sorry I'm too much to fly with."

"No trouble, just more time," Judellie said.

"Well, uh," Tenver offered, "I can push the grass out of your way, I suppose?"

Judellie agreed and Chive wriggled like a shrug. So Tenver lolloped ahead, his nose ploughing the grass. Judellie's footfalls crackled behind him; they set out like that, south-westbound toward town.

Running needed all four of Tenver's paws so he held the eggshell bundle with his mouth, a corner of the cotton clamped tight in his teeth. The scent of home filled him each time he inhaled. He wanted to be back there, wanted to see Constezza's face ignite with joy and feel her touch soothe his neck. As Tenver thought of rock-walled places, and he heard only fragments of Chive's chattering to Judellie.

"I don't like baking," Chive said at one point, "and it doesn't much like me, either. The yeast loves Sage — but, oh, no, it won't listen to *my* plantcasting. So why struggle at it, I supposed? Why not make a different contribution? Bring back sweetleaf for the cakes, or chicory for the biscuits? That's all well and good — but still, any forager can find sweetleaf or chicory, you see? I thought if I could bring back something grand like a heap of salt crystal ... I don't know."

"You could make a name for yourself?" Judellie offered.

"No! Well, yes ... For the whole Newwin family, or maybe all of Plainsreach."

"Hmm," Judellie said.

The tone of her voice was familiar. Not familiar like Judellie of Cherez, but familiar like any korvi friend sighing to voice her fatigue. Tenver stopped and turned back toward her: Judellie held Chive high but her own posture was slumping, like she melted from her own firecasting-stoked movement.

He dropped the eggshells into his hands to free his mouth. "Are you well? Maybe I should go ahead and get someone else to help."

Judellie inhaled: she wanted to protest, but good sense glimmered in her eyes like water at night. "You should. I will keep going, but ..."

"I'll go ahead, I can ask someone strong to meet you partway." The mage would surely know who to recruit.

"Tell them I'm sorry for the trouble," Chive said. Hanging there in the sling, she craned to see Tenver. She flinched when her delicate antennae brushed the leather's edge but she wore earnestness on her face all the same. "Tell them it'll be worth the while, please."

Tenver gave her a nod of promise. Then he hung the eggshells from his clamped teeth and ran, darting through the grass and flareflowers and daisy stems.

He had another goal to run toward — but the bundle he held still smelled like somewhere else, and Tenver's thoughts wafted away while he ran.

When he was still small and his adult fur was growing in reluctant, Constezza first told him the legend of korvi's wings. She still told it often, with korvi eggs listening as well. It was a tale of ancient times, thousands of generations ago when the gods had first granted magic and everyone was new. Korvi people wanted arms and legs and wings, so they went out and got them. Even when it was frightening and frustrating. Even when the effort hurt.

Constezza wore the oddest smile while she first told him that tale — an expression Tenver hadn't understood at the time, but had etched into his memory for later. Now, Tenver was sure that his mother liked that particular legend. She was fond of that story-told fellow who saw the sky beyond his reach and leaped toward it. She must have hoped that a healer nursed that fool from so long ago, minding his injuries while they knitted.

Constezza was surely worrying about Tenver right now, he knew with a stone sinking in his gut. She woke up to an empty home this day — not a lonely home, since she had the eggs to talk to, but still quiet as a cave's depths. Even if she knew Tenver planned to leave, that still wasn't fair. And in this very moment, she had no inkling where Tenver was. He should have at least told her goodbye. But the choice was made.

Running began to jar his bones. It was a relief to see Plainsreach buildings rise over the grass tops.

The Plainsreach mage did know precisely who to recruit: an enormously tall korvi man, as broad and yellow as the sky, with paint smudges on his arms from whatever he had been working on. He leaped into the air and was gone. Tenver explained Chive's trouble to the mage — and keeping Chive lying still had been a wise bet, if the worried blankness on the mage's face was any measure of it.

Soon enough, voices rose in the street, a mosaic of worry. The big korvi man carried Chive in her sling — carried her into the mage home, toward the mage whose hands glowed with readied brightcasting. Judellie rejoined Tenver outside the mage's door, and she breathed hard but she wore a smile frayed from use.

"There! We did it, friend."

Holding the eggshell bundle close in his arms, Tenver nodded. "Chive must be glad that we did."

Inclining her head, like she might peek through solid cotton wrapping, Judellie asked, "Constezza's shells are ...?"

"Yeah, they're all here. And they're not broken any more than Constezza broke them herself — I checked." He shifted on his haunches. "Do you think you can fly back to Hotrock today? If you're too tired, that's all right, but ... She must be thinking of me."

Without hesitation, Judellie looked to the sky, to the particular shade of yellow afternoon. "I think so. Just give me a few moments, I would like a meal. Something for fuel, you see?"

"Of course."

She turned toward the market street.

"Wait," Tenver blurted, "Judellie? Could I have my blanket back? It's in the carrying pouch."

It took her a blinking moment to recall the carrying pouch she wore. But she bent and gave Tenver back his other knotted bundle.

"I'm going to wait here," he said. "To see if Chive's healing goes well."

Judellie nodded. "You must be hungry, as well. What do you like?"

"Anything is fine. Something with firebuds chopped into it, if you can."

She was gone a moment later; it took Tenver that long to untie his blanket and put his trade trinkets off to one corner. The rest of the blanket he smoothed out over the bare street dirt, a stone's throw from the mage's door. It wasn't as colourful as a bard's blanket ought to be, but the movement still caught attention: passing aemets slowed their feet and came nearer. One called to another to fetch the children, so they could hear, too.

Tenver walked two-footed into the very middle of the blanket. He kept making hasty decisions, just bolting off into new arrangements like he was still birth-blind — but this particular new thing couldn't possibly be a bad idea.

"Everyone," he said in his loudest voice, "I'm Tenver Lightling, call me Tenver. And I don't usually tell legends like this. But I learned something today, so I think I should share it with everybody. Sharing legends is how we all know what to do — isn't that right?"

It sounded like pure clumsiness in Tenver's ears. But the gathered faces were all mild, and a few nodded like crumbs of encouragement. A ferrin face poked in between other folk's legs. The aemet children arrived at the edge of the gathering, tiny folk with stick-thin limbs and deer's wary eyes.

With his electricity so calm he could barely believe it, Tenver held himself tall, and he began: "Once, a few hours ago in this very land, there was a ferrin. And he made a mistake."

He stumbled through his legend, tripping on the gaps where he left out Constezza's good name, pausing often to grab more thoughts. A few people drifted away; a few more arrived. Judellie joined the gathering's edge, her tall redness standing out stark against the aemet folk.

"And that ferrin learned," Tenver ventured, "he learned that ... Sometimes you can slip up and still get some good from it, as long as you don't just let the mistake lie there. And any moment can be the moment you decide to give something a fire-hearted try. And ... maybe the next thing you try will be the right one." He let his courage finally go, and his ears finally wilt. "Um. Thanks for listening."

Murmurs rose from the crowd, a small-voiced chorus. The mass of folk splintered apart, wandering back to daily life. But half a dozen folk must have sieved some value out of Tenver's story: they retrieved things from their pockets and pouches and carrying baskets, and bent to place them on Tenver's blanket.

"If you've got any," Tenver asked, "I'd like green herbs, please. Wholesome vegetable things. They're for someone."

One aemet hesitated, took her handful of payment back and produced a knuckle-wide bundle of spinach for Tenver instead. An earned token to bring home.

In the settling calm afterward, with his blanket folded up unobtrusive and the Plainsreach townsfolk carrying on past him, Tenver took his meal. Judellie had brought him a wedge of onion-studded corn bread, and a juice-heavy apple. Nothing had ever tasted so good in his life.

"You have a good skill for words," Judellie said. She perched beside him, knees folded, watching the peoplekind river flow past.

Tenver swallowed a last gulp of hard-edged apple core. "I'm not sure if it's a skill, or if I just keep having good luck."

"I think it is a skill. But a skill that gets better the more you do it, maybe."

"Lots of things are like that. Well, for what it's worth, you have a skill for travelling."

Judellie nodded — gradually, while plans gathered behind her eyes.

Chive emerged from the mage home not long after, hung again in the sling and carried by the yellow-feathered korvi. She was well and talkative — mostly about how the salt should have warded off any rot demon that might be eyeing her wound. She thanked the two of them again.

"You're welcome to visit," she added as she was carried away. "If you need some salt, you know a friend who's got it!"

That would be a point to remember, Tenver supposed, the next time he readied himself to barter.

There was one more long flight to endure, with the pouch cramping Tenver and the wind clawing through the cloth. This flight he didn't mind so much — not when he had his bundled-up goal in his arms.

He hopped out of the pouch more carefully, landing on tunnelstreet rock with three stumbling feet. And he looked up at Judellie, who held her wings fanned wide still.

"I want to tell Tijo the message," she said.

"Oh, that's right." A trade of metal for spinach, however folk chose to word it. "You remember the whole message, right?"

"Yes! If the words bite my rump again, I will bring you back to Tijo, maybe." She grinned, looking every bit strong and grown. "Tell Constezza good day for me, yes?"

Tenver surely would.

He ran home on four feet, nearly flying. Home would smell like the eggshell bundle except steeped richer, a smell of feathers and fire and spice-touched dinner. Only the pulling of Tenver's ferrin gut made him notice neighbours in the tunnels: he recalled belated that their eyes widened when they saw him.

Longwick Clan home was empty. Constezza was out in the tunnelstreets somewhere — but the hearth was full of cool ashes. All of the egg nests gaped, empty.

Tenver didn't understand. He put down his blanket satchel, and put the eggshell bundle in the storage box where it belonged, and he kept running, searching with his ears held high.

Constezza's voice wasn't chiming warm in any neighbour's homes. Her amber colouring and bright-stitched wingsleeve weren't in the market street. Tenver was halfway down the path to the stream outside, imagining her fetching some simple water, when the healer korvi caught up to him. She had that terrible wideness in her eyes before she explained.

Tenver didn't notice anything else in the numbness afterward. The pyre was prepared already, piled high with wood and coal, draped with a shroud. Everyone had waited for him, the most necessary friend for this funeral.

Constezza seemed fine this morning, the healer had said. *Saw us for a flask of tonic. Said she was just a little tired. A neighbour found her two hours later, cool and barely awake. Her flame faded so fast. We tried.*

At least she had her eggshells, Tenver thought while he watched the pyre burn and leap and vanish into ashen earth. He shivered and barely noticed the air-thin condolences spoken around him, and he regretted everything with a wholeness he could have fallen into. But at least Constezza had herself back.

It wasn't from any demon I've ever known. These things come right out of the yellow, sometimes. We'll all miss her terribly. Great Fyrian will be good to her — and bless your heart for finding those shells.

Longwick Clan home smelled ever so slightly of other people's casting. A trace at the back of Tenver's throat, like a memory. It faded over the next day and night, while Tenver sat watching the hearth coals' wavering colours. The korvi eggs were back in their hearthside nests: Tenver agreed to tend them, because their parents had jobs to do and Tenver now had nothing.

"Tenver?" Judellie's korvi accent came from outside the door. "Are you here?"

"Yeah."

She came in with a flap of the door curtain. Sticks clattered onto the woodpile.

"Thank you," Tenver said. "You can take something, if you'd like."

She came closer, careful feet nearly soundless on the carpet. "I heard, just today. I am— I'm so sorry."

Tenver just looked at his feet under his sarong's edge.

"I ... wanted to thank you," Judellie said, quiet, "for bringing me on that journey. Chive is mending well. She asked if I would run some errand flights for her, so ... I will be going away to make trades. Everywhere in the land, maybe."

At least Judellie had found the whole fluff-brained chase to be useful. Tenver sat facing the flickering fire, and tried to lift his ears for Judellie, for her good news. They shifted a little, too heavy to move freely.

"Do you need any other things? Before I go?"

"No, thank you."

A silence passed, like melting stone. Feathers slid in Judellie's shifting wings.

She spoke and Tenver's mind jumped to keep pace, to pull apart the korvitongue words: "*Constezza was a flame that touched the sky, and you're a spark the very same-burning. She is proud of you still. So ... maybe this challenge gave you a truth-knowledge.*"

Wisdom, Tenver supposed. The closest translation was wisdom. And he did need to find some wisdom in all of this. If he could spin a legend out of this whole sorry happenstance, his mother would never truly fade away.

In the molten quiet, Judellie bent over him, and her hand was a sudden, kind weight on his back. Tenver jumped, finding recognition in the same heartbeat he met her dark eyes. Who would have thought that a ferrin's four-year life was long enough to smelt the truth?

"*You'll maybe-need people,*" she said lightly. Then, in ordinary commontongue, "Ask folk for help while I am gone, you hear me?"

"I won't have to worry about that. The Joivennes brought me a whole day's worth of meals." He managed a shard of a smile. "They said they'll cook me a pan bread in the depth of night, if I want. I don't think I'll ask for that much. But still ... Thank you."

With a parting rub, a slightest ruffling of his fur, Judellie rose. The room was brighter even after she was gone.

Tenver stayed sitting at the hearth fire, and shadows still flickered around him. The eggs sat with him. He was barely larger than these unhatched korvi, and he had no fire inside him, and he didn't even like the feel of flying. But Tenver Lightling, call him Tenver, was the child of a korvi. He was the only member of Longwick Clan now.

He rose to two feet. He turned one egg, then the other, each one a warm enormity that his arms didn't fit all the way around. He sat again and watched shadows quiver on the eggs' shells. He bowed his head.

"I suppose you'll want to hear peopletongues." He glanced at the Iliyan egg, the one that would quicken any day now. "You, particularly."

There was no answer. Tenver rubbed his furred face in both hands.

It might help to talk to them, the good Iliyan had said when she set her egg down. *No one listens like a child in shell.*

It might help to talk to them, and besides, Tenver needed to tell Constezza's legend to these unhatched korvi. He knew those two truths like the ache of a sealed old cut. He drew a breath and — after deciding which tongue to use first — he began.

"Not long ago," he said, "in a Volcano town the very same as this one, there was a korvi woman named Constezza of Veliere. You knew her, in a way. Maybe you remember her voice."

The home's quiet had changed already, less stifling but still full of care. Tenver could tell Constezza's whole legend and the story of *ten, ten* within it. He was dragon enough to do that much.

Heidi C. Vlach thanks you, the reader, for your time and interest. Sharing stories is what gives them meaning.

To learn more about Heidi and her fantasy writing, visit www.heidicvlach.com.

If you enjoyed Tenver and Constezza's story, you might be interested in the other *Stories of Aligare*. Each book is a stand-alone story with different main characters.

Remedy

A novel of medical drama. Deaf korvi Peregrine wants his ferrin assistant Tillian to live her own life. But when plague strikes an aemet village, Peregrine and Tillian must separate to lend their aid — whether Peregrine is ready or not.

Ravel

A romantic novelette. Aster has the ideal life for a young aemet woman: family, career and tradition. Then comes the merry korvi bard, Llarez. He sparks the thoughts of freedom Aster has never known what to do with.

Render

A mystery novel. Rue is a young aemet coming of age in a misfortune-fraught mountain community. When wolves start hunting aemets for food, Rue promises herself she'll solve the village's problems. She'll need help from Felixi, a korvi game hunter — but Felixi knows more than he's willing to share.

Made in the USA
Charleston, SC
08 April 2014